THE RAINBOW CHRONICLES

A Story of Hope for Today

Dave Pipitone

Third Edition

This is a work of fiction. All names, characters, places and events are works of imagination of the author and do not refer to real life situations.

All rights reserved. No part of this book may be reproduced or transmitted in any form or by any means, electronic or mechanical, including photocopying, recording or by any information storage and retrieval system, without the written permission of the author. The quote in Chapter 16 is a rephrased version of Ezekiel 33:11.

Illustrations by Dave Pipitone; children and rainbow for Forever a Family, www.depositphotos.com

Third Edition

Copyright © 2022 Dave Pipitone

Transforming Life Press LLC, Kissimmee, FL

Geegee,
Thanks for being the AMAZING AUNT & Godmother that you are! Love, Dave

For teens and their families everywhere: may your deep and perfect love bring more peace to our world, making it a better place to live.

CONTENTS

Epigraph	VII
Prologue	IX
1. In The Village	1
2. At The King's Fortress	11
3. Journey's Beginning	19
4. In A Strange Land	31
5. Making New Friends	42
6. At The Governor's Feast	50
7. Traveling Through The Countryside	59
8. Secrets To Keep	70
9. Entering The Purple Door	80
10. Crossing Paths	90
11. Trials On The Journey	100
12. Reaching The Summit	111
13. A Kiss For The Tulips	117

14.	At The Rainbow's End	126
15.	A War Over The Flowers	137
16.	The Return Of The Rainbow	146
What's Coming Next?		156
List of Characters		160
Thanks		163
About the Author		165

Creation is groaning and calls for rebirth, A new world is blooming for all life on earth. The Spirit of Wisdom is hovering above: *"Bring Your family together, unite us in Love."*

Verse One, *Forever a Family*

PROLOGUE

Once upon a time, in a land far away, there was a Kingdom where all was right and good. It was a magnificent place. The land was like a lush garden. The people were blessed with abundance and peace. Everything and everyone was in touch with the Throne of the Almighty. The Rainbow spanned the sky and touched both ends of the Kingdom, east and west.

Then, one day, trouble struck. Half of the Rainbow was stolen and disappeared, the side that touched the east part of the land. The land in the east became desolate and was named Eregon. One end of the Rainbow still rested in the land in the west, which flourished and became known as Neer'stazone.

The right and good of the Kingdom stayed with Eregon. Yet, even with the Rainbow's End touching it, Neer'stazone held a dark, sinister secret locked deep within the land. That division was never intended by The Almighty, Who created the Great River to separate and protect the two peoples until the land could be restored. And so our story begins...

Chapter One
In the Village

"Gramma!"

"Gramma, please help me!"

Rosalina ran to Wilby's room and entered. Wilby was half-asleep.

"Wake up, Wilby! What is it?" Rosalina asked.

"Gramma, it's the dream again."

"The dream about the big chair?" Rosalina sat down on Wilby's bed.

"Yes, that one," said Wilby. "The big chair in a large room, with so many different faces and people. But it was so different this time."

"What was so different?"

"It's like the chair was so high, almost in the sky. There was such a bright light that I could hardly see. And that light came from the chair. There was all this music, people laughing, and so many things I've never seen before around the chair. I felt terrified, Gramma."

"It's just a dream, dear." Rosalina hugged Wilby and stroked her hair. "Maybe it's time to get up now. I have to finish something."

"What is it, Gramma?"

"The final stitches of my needlepoint," Rosalina whispered.

Earlier that day, the village baker was about to close his shop, when Rhima walked in.

"Do you have any more wheat bread to sell, Andrew?" Rhima squinted through the empty glass shelves in the village bakery.

"Rhima, you always wait until the end of the day to see what's left. I have one loaf left in the back, that I planned to take home for my family."

"Would you mind splitting it with me? I ran out yesterday and have been so busy putting away the latest purses, that I couldn't get here earlier."

"Oh...yes, I'll give you half, Rhima."

Andrew sighed as he retrieved the loaf. He eyed the middle of the loaf and cut the bread in half.

"Perfect!" said Rhima. "Thank you so much for sharing what you have with me."

"It's been another long day, in a rough year, year after year," mused Andrew. ""But yes, you're welcome. Please come earlier tomorrow, Rhima."

"I'll be here first thing in the morning, Andrew. Thanks again."

"Have a good night, I'm closing up now."

Rhima walked out the front door and Andrew locked it after her.

A half-day before Wilby had her dream, a distance away, soldiers' torches lit the forest road as they traveled at dusk. It was the same dusk every day. The torch flames flickered, casting shadows on the barren trees and ground.

Cargas and Lemet, two of the King's best cavalry, led the search party for Wilby, who lived in the village of Hdora. As they neared the Great Open Space in the Forest, Cargas paused to rest.

"When will the rain come, so we can go home?" Lemet asked.

Cargas grunted. "There is only this dry gray veil that covers the sky. Gray and parched, like the land."

"It has been years since I've last felt the rain," Lemet sighed. "Things were so different then, with the green grass, the abundant crops, the colorful flowers, and the Great Waterfall. And after the rain came the Rainbow—"

"Stop!" cried Cargas. "You know that we are under strict orders not to recall its name."

"Sorry, so sorry," apologized Lemet.

The two scouts became silent as they continued their journey through the Great Forest. Their torches reflected from the dusty road, sending shadows across the Great Open Space as they left the Forest.

This space was so alive once with green plants and flowers, a magnificent meadow, thought Cargas. *It is a shame to live in such a barren land now.*

As night fell, the sky stayed cloudy, and no stars shone. But at the other end of the Great Open Space, pinpricks of light shone steadily at the horizon.

There are the lights of Hdora, thought Lemet. *I've never been there. I remember the stories about the grand borders and beds of flowers that once grew here. Hdora was the prettiest village in Eregon.*

Lemet and Cargas rode on in silence and approached the gates of Hdora. Cargas dismounted, walked to the entryway, and rang the gong. "Open up, for the King!" he shouted.

A watchman appeared from the tower and hailed them, "Who is there? What do you want?"

"We are Cargas and Lemet, from the King's Royal troops. We seek Wilby of Hdora," cried Cargas.

The watchman hurried down the steps and removed the bar from the gate. As the gate groaned open, Cargas, Lemet, and the rest of the search party rode into the village courtyard. They reined their horses and came to a stop in front of the village square's dried-up flowerbed.

"We came in search of Wilby," Cargas declared. "Where is he?"

The village folk had heard the commotion and gathered in front of the courthouse. "Wilby?" they asked. "Wilby? There is no man or boy named Wilby here in Hdora. But there is a teenage girl named Wilby, who lives with her grandmother."

Cargas was dismayed. "Wilby is a girl?"

"What do you want with a teenager, especially with Wilby?" asked Rhima, the village purse peddler. "She is precious to us. Has she done something wrong?"

"You soldiers are always taking something or someone," exclaimed Andrew, the village baker. "We never learn what happens. Now, you want to take Wilby, one of our best joys, away from us!"

The muttering crowd formed a circle around the horses. "Wait!" cried Lemet. "We are here on a mission from the King! He has a special task for the person named Wilby of Hdora."

"Quiet, Lemet," ordered Cargas. "I'll handle this. Don't forget your rank." He addressed the crowd, "Have no fear! We are on a peaceful mission. The King needs Wilby because of his, er, her special gifts."

"Peaceful mission?" argued Rhima. "Is that what you're about? Aren't armies trained for war, not peace?"

"I have no time to debate with you," said Cargas. "Tell us where to find Wilby, and we'll be on our way."

The crowd stood silently for some time. Finally, Rhima said, "Wilby lives in the house at the end of the lilac street. It is over there, past the courthouse."

"Thank you!" Cargas and the cavalry wheeled their horses toward the lilac street.

Soon they came to a small, well-kept cottage. The remains of a hedge surrounded what had once been a garden in front. Inside, Wilby was awake and reading by the fire. Rosalina held up a colorful needlepoint.

"It's done, finally," said Rosalina, holding the canvas in front of her. "What do you think of it?"

"Oh, that's beautiful, Gramma!" said Wilby, looking up from her book. She was a girl of about fourteen with brown hair and gray eyes. "I see a little girl standing in a field of colorful things. But what are they, and what are those stripes of color that stretch across the sky in the distance?"

"Well the colorful things in the field are flowers, dear. The color comes from the petals."

"What are petals, Gramma?"

"Petals are what bloom from a flower. A flower is a green plant with roots, a stem, and leaves. As the flower grows, it forms buds, like a little ball. The buds get larger and one day, they open up - they blossom - and a flower is born. The petals show the color of the flower."

"Are there different types of flowers?"

"Yes! The Almighty made many different sizes, shapes, and colors of flowers. There are flower blossoms with five, six, eight, or even twenty petals. Some say that a field of flowers is like seeing the glory - the majesty of The Almighty."

Wilby took a deep breath. "This is so amazing."

"Flowers are amazing, Wilby. In this needlepoint, the little girl is you, standing in a patch of tulips." Rosalina paused. "Oh, that's right, you probably don't remember what tulips looked like. Your father grew them here, years ago. And in the background, that's the Rainbow."

"Gramma, I don't remember my father." Wilby sighed. "I wish I had known him. So many other children played and danced with their fathers. I missed all of that..."

After a few moments, she continued. "Where were the tulips my father grew?"

"The tulips grew all over the village. Among all the villages of the Kingdom, Hdora was noted for its beautiful flowers. There were tulips, irises, lilacs, and so many more. Your father was loved and respected by everyone. He led the other gardeners in the village and inspired them to create this beauty. The tulip is your birth flower, Wilby."

"My birth flower? What is that?"

"A birth flower is a flower your father chooses when you are born. Some fathers use the standard flower that gardeners assign to a specific month. But not your father. He was soft-hearted. He chose a tulip."

"Why did he choose a tulip, Gramma?"

"A tulip has a special meaning. Tulips mean deep and perfect love. Your father saw that in you when you were born, Wilby. He used to call you his little tulip. He hoped that one day you would do something very special, something that showed your deep and perfect love."

"Really? When will that be, Gramma?"

"Only The Almighty knows, Wilby. I will tell you this, a tulip has six petals that grow like a cup, a closed hand. At your father's house, on the day you were born, a dark-purple tulip opened all six petals, like an open hand stretching out in all directions - to the sky, the land, and all around. They say that happens once in a lifetime."

"But where is my father now? Did he die?"

"I don't know. He left home and I haven't seen him for many years."

"Why did he leave, Gramma?"

"I'm so sorry, Wilby. I can't tell you that."

"And the colored stripes in the sky you called a Rainbow, I don't remember seeing the Rainbow."

"That was in the age before. And the Rainbow didn't look exactly like this. One end was ..."

There was a scuffle of feet outside and a loud knock on the door. "Open the door!" a voice cried. "Open in the name of the King!"

Rosalina flew to the door and peeped through its window. Cargas, Lemet, and the scouting party dismounted and huddled outside. She undid the latch and opened the door.

"I am Rosalina. What business do you have, scaring my granddaughter and me this late at night?"

"We're sorry, ma'am," said Lemet. "You see, we're on the King's business to find Wilby, and—"

"Lemet!" Cargas interrupted. "Keep quiet! I'll handle this." He turned toward Rosalina. "I'm sorry, ma'am. It is late. If our mission were not urgent, we would have waited until morning. May I come in, please?"

Rosalina opened the door wider, and Cargas entered the cottage.

Wilby came forward. Wilby wore a plain dress and carried an air of confidence. "I am Wilby," she said. "What do you want from me?"

"You are Wilby?" replied Lemet, peering in from the doorway.

"Lemet!" fumed Cargas through clenched teeth.

"I am Wilby. What do you want?"

"Wilby, my name is Cargas, chief cavalry officer to the King, whose throne rules from the Fortress City." He reached into the sack he was carrying, took out a Scroll, and unrolled it. He found his place and read:

"The good King of Eregon, a man of virtue and honor, hereby requests the favor of Wilby, of the town of Hdora, to visit the Fortress City and save the Kingdom from its troubling conditions."

Cargas rolled up the Scroll and put it back into the sack. Rosalina raised her eyebrows and then narrowed her eyes. "Now you want my granddaughter, too! Wasn't my son enough?"

"I don't know anything about your son, Rosalina," replied Cargas. "I have come to bring Wilby to the King."

"He's really a good man, the King," blurted out Lemet. "So they say, anyway."

Cargas glared coldly at Lemet.

"Sorry, so sorry," Lemet muttered.

"We don't want to force Wilby to go with us," said Cargas, stretching his body to its full height. "After all, it's an invitation from the King."

"I'll go, Gramma," said Wilby. "I am of age; I will find out what the King wants of me. You told me that I was born to do something special, to show my deep and perfect love. Maybe this is it."

Rosalina gazed at her granddaughter. *She is so young, so innocent, to get mixed up in the Kingdom's affairs.*

"Let me speak to Wilby alone," she said.

"We'll wait outside," said Cargas. "Be brief."

"Wilby, I raised you from birth," Rosalina said. "I know that you are special, so wise for your age. I will let you go if you wish to go."

"Gramma, I will go and find out what the King wants of me." Wilby walked to her room and packed a bag with clothing, a brush, and extra shoes. She returned to the living room and hugged Rosalina. "I'll miss you so." Wilby wiped a tear from Gramma's eye.

"I'll miss you, too," whispered Rosalina. "Let me give you a piece of advice. Things on a journey don't always go as planned. There are times when you have to scriggle."

"Scriggle?" said Wilby.

"Yes, scriggle. Try something different, do something new. Zig instead of zagging. Wiggle a little or zag a lot. Don't get stuck in only one way of thinking or doing something."

"Okay, Gramma, I'll remember that."

"Look at you! You're growing up. Your personal adventure is starting. Oh, the things you will discover! May you travel safely with the breath of The Almighty."

Wilby went out of the cottage and mounted the horse that Lemet showed her.

"May the blessing of The Almighty go with you, Wilby," Rosalina called after them as they galloped down the lilac street.

The scouting party rode out of the village and into the Great Forest. Wilby clung to the spotted white horse she was riding. Lemet led the way, and Cargas rode by her side; the rest of the party followed behind them. They rode for two nights and a day.

Finally, the party arrived at the Fortress City shortly before midnight. The massive stone walls were ablaze with torches. The gate towered above them as the drawbridge lowered to meet them. The party entered the Fortress courtyard and dismounted.

"Tomorrow morning, you'll meet the King," Cargas told Wilby. "I'll show you to your room now."

They entered the Fortress and climbed a long flight of stairs. Cargas led Wilby to a small chamber in the middle of a dimly lit hallway. Tylma, a chambermaid, was waiting there.

"Greetings, Wilby!" she said. "Here are some fresh clothes, bath soap, and a warm bed. If you need anything, my room is next door."

"Thank you. I can use these things." Wilby was tired after the long ride. Tylma and Cargas left, locking the door behind them. Wilby washed, changed clothes, and crashed on the bed. Within minutes, she was sound asleep.

Chapter Two

At the King's Fortress

Bang! Bang!

The door to Wilby's room shook with the sound. It was about nine in the morning. The door shuddered as it swung open.

Kilmaz, Captain of the King's Guard, stood there. "Wake up, Wilby! You are to see the King now," he announced. "Get your things."

Wilby got up, took her sack, and followed Kilmaz up a tall stairway and down a long hallway. The hallway emptied into the Great Hall, a large room with a high ceiling and richly paneled walls.

A long, rectangular wooden table was in the middle of the room, surrounded by many chairs. A large throne was at one end of the table, intricately carved and inlaid with gold and silver.

"Wait here, Wilby," stated Kilmaz. He left the room through a paneled door that appeared from nowhere.

Wilby wandered near the table and traced lines in the thick coat of dust that covered it. It had not been used for some time. *This chair reminds me of my dream, just not as big,* thought Wilby.

Shortly, Kilmaz reappeared with two figures behind him. He stopped and knelt.

"Sire, this is Wilby," he said to the first figure, who was dressed in black.

"Ah, Wilby!" said the King. "I've been looking forward to meeting you." The King walked to the giant throne and sat down.

"It is an honor, O King. That sure is a big chair!" Bowing low, Wilby peeked at the King. He had a short gray beard, sad eyes, and a stooped back.

"Let's get down to business! We're wasting time on pleasantries," interrupted the second figure, who wore a long brown robe and a large, pointed hat. "We're here to talk about the Rainbow's End."

"Seer, can't you wait for anything?" said the King. "Wilby, we brought you here for a reason. Come with me. I want to show you something."

The King walked to a panel in the wall and pressed it. The panel slid down, and a window appeared. "Look out and tell me what you see."

"Well, I see roads and dirt," replied Wilby. "Some people are standing, traveling, and working down there. Off to the left, I see a large forest. There is the endless gray sky, like always. It looks like what I normally see, only a lot smaller."

"You're three hundred feet from the ground, Wilby!" said the Seer. "Of course, things look small."

"What colors do you see?" asked the King.

"Different types of brown, and some gray, too," responded Wilby. "Just like at home in the village."

"Oh, stop this rubbish!" The Seer frowned at the King. "Are you going to talk about the mission, or am I?"

"I'm building up to it," replied the King. "Wilby, our land of Eregon is in trouble. We need to remove that trouble so we can prosper again. All of the brown and gray you see was once a large garden covering the entire Kingdom. Flowers flourished, along with crops of wheat and corn. Trees had many different shapes, sizes, and shades of green leaves. This was at that blessed time when the Rainbow's End, a sign of The Almighty's blessing, rested upon our land."

"My grandmother said that my father grew flowers, too," replied Wilby. "She even showed me a picture of me in a patch of tulips, with the Rainbow in the distance."

The Seer added, "The King is right. One of the Rainbow's Ends was here. The ancient Scrolls say that one end of the Rainbow is wrapped around The Almighty's Throne. We only see it disappear into the clouds. The Rainbow is always in The Almighty's presence; it links the land to The Almighty. The Rainbow's End blesses whatever land it touches. The Rainbow itself is not The Almighty, but it brings the presence of The Almighty to the world. Without that presence, the land is in chaos."

"Now, we've seen those effects here," said the King. "No Rainbow's End! Instead, we have famine, dryness, unrest, and great distress among the people. In a word, gloom. We need to get the Rainbow's End back!"

"Did you say 'back,' sire?" asked Wilby.

"Yes, I said 'back.' Wilby, when the Rainbow's End touched our land, we were blessed among the kingdoms of the earth. Many peoples looked to us for assistance and paid tribute. But then one day, enemies, *spies*, came into our land and stole the Rainbow's End."

"I remember that day well," added the Seer. "We enjoyed the light and warmth of the sun. But there was one Kingdom, then, not many kingdoms. The trouble began to happen immediately when the Rainbow's End left our land. The Great Waterfall dried up. Then the other Kingdom arose. Now gray skies cover our land and hover over the people."

"Yes, well, history is not my specialty, wizard!" the King said. "The Rainbow's End would often appear at the end of a storm, after the rain, when the sun broke through the clouds."

"What is rain, sire?" asked Wilby.

"Rain?" exclaimed the Seer. "You've never experienced rain? Double hmmph!"

"I still don't know what rain is," giggled Wilby.

"Well, all right; rain is made of thousands of drops of water that fall from the sky," said the Seer. "Sometimes, it's gentle; sometimes, it's violent. How the rain comes often depends on the wind."

"At one time, the Rainbow's End came only after it rained," the Seer continued. "Then, the Great Waterfall appeared under the Rainbow's End, with enough water for the entire land. The rain stopped, but the Rainbow's End still touched the land. That colored air is gone now."

The King interrupted, "In Neer'stazone, where you will be going, there are no clouds, only clear, blue sky. It doesn't rain at all, yet the Rainbow's End is still there. It is in the distance, beyond the Great Mountain."

"This story is amazing." Wilby was bewildered by all of this talk. "Who were these thieves who stole the Rainbow's End?"

The Seer stared at the King and said tersely, "You know who that was. It was—"

"Quiet!" The King cut the Seer off. "Those names are never to be mentioned or remembered here or anywhere else. As King, I forbid it!"

He turned to the girl. "Wilby, this is your mission," decreed the King. "You must go to the Kingdom of Neer'stazone and bring the Rainbow's End back to our land. We must have The Almighty's blessing and not this chaos."

"How can I do such a thing?" replied Wilby. "This is so different! I don't know where to go or how to get there. And if I should find this Rainbow's End, how would I bring it back? Would I tell this color to go where I say or drag it back with a rope?"

"Ah, you ask such good questions," remarked the Seer. "No, Wilby, you cannot force the Rainbow's End to return to us by physical means. The Rainbow's End is connected to The Almighty's Throne. It is only through entering it with a pure heart and an intention for well-being that you can reach The Almighty's ear. Then, the Rainbow's End will come home to us."

"So, I must enter the Rainbow's End and talk to The Almighty?" asked Wilby.

"Yes, yes, yes! But you must talk with your heart, not with words. Let your heart hold no meanness, no thought of yourself. Think of others and of the blessings the Rainbow's End will bring to our land. You are entering holy ground when you touch the Rainbow's End."

Then the King brought out a small chest covered with jewels of every color. The Seer reached deep into a front robe pocket and retrieved a small key made of purple crystal.

The King opened the chest and removed a white amulet about the size of a teacup saucer that had a raised rim around its outer edge. A series of engraved arcs was at the center—six curved lines evenly spaced. The King handed the amulet to Wilby.

"When you reach Neer'stazone, you must put this on, Wilby," said the King. "The white amulet will protect you and hide your identity from those in Neer'stazone who would wish to stop you. We are different people from them. As you get closer to the Rainbow's End, people will ask you where you come from and where you are going. You must keep your mission a secret; tell no one. Never, under any circumstances, remove the amulet or reveal your secret."

The Seer added, "The amulet will guide you to the Rainbow's End. With the amulet on, you can think your thoughts to The Almighty. As you journey, these engraved lines will become the colors of the Rainbow's End. The last color to appear will be purple. Then you will know that it is time to enter the Rainbow's End."

"Why is purple the last color?" asked Wilby.

"Oh, don't you know anything?" snapped the Seer. "Purple is the closest color to The Almighty. I've studied the ancient writings, which reveal the truth."

"The Almighty's Throne rests on twelve layers of precious stones. The twelfth layer is amethyst, which is purple. We believe that purple is the color of the Rainbow's End that is wrapped closest to the Throne. That's why purple is the highest color of the

AT THE KING'S FORTRESS

Rainbow's End. It is the color closest to the heavens where The Almighty dwells."

"But I don't know where to find the Rainbow's End!" exclaimed Wilby. "How will I know that I am going in the right direction or walking on the right path?"

The King answered, "Look on the other side of the Great Mountain, which is toward the eastern edge of Neer'stazone. The wind will act as a messenger. It blows at different times and with different strengths, from the rustling of a gentle breeze to strong, rock-rending gusts. Learn to listen to the wisdom of the wind. The wind and the amulet will guide you."

"Yes, yes," the Seer cut in. "The amulet and the wind can guide you, but they are on the outside. Sometimes the wind carries the breath of The Almighty."

He poked Wilby in the chest. "Listen also to what's inside of you; your heart will speak to you. Hunches, promptings, dreams, feelings, people who appear at the right time to help you—all of them come from the breath of The Almighty."

"What about food?" asked Wilby. "Where will I sleep? I don't even know anyone where I'm going."

"Just follow your mission, Wilby," said the Seer. "Everything you need will appear as you need it."

"Am I to go alone?" Wilby asked.

The King sighed. "This is *your* mission, Wilby. Your personal adventure. No one else can do this for you. However, you may have a guide who will lead you through the borderlands."

"May Lemet go with me?" Wilby inquired. "Please, let Lemet come."

"Lemet? Lemet? Who is Lemet?"

"He came with a group of your men to my village of Hdora. I like him."

"Well, all right," conceded the King. "Lemet may go with you until you reach the Great River. Now be on your way, Wilby! We've had enough talk; it's time for action."

He motioned the captain of the Royal Guard to escort Wilby out. Wilby returned to her room and slipped the amulet into her backpack. Cargas led her to the courtyard, where she mounted the spotted horse. Lemet was waiting.

"It looks like a good day for a ride," said Lemet. His voice was cheerful. "Let's go!"

They rode out of the castle and headed west toward the Age-Old Road. The King and the Seer watched Wilby and Lemet shrink toward the horizon at the window. "Do you think Wilby can do it?" asked the King. "She is a girl, you know."

"I do have my doubts," said the Seer. "Yet everything I've read and know points to her as the one to restore the Rainbow's End to us. I hope that I am hearing The Almighty correctly about this."

"I hope so, too," said the King. "I hope she's not like her father."

Kilmaz entered the Throne Room and approached the King, "Sire, shall I seize the picture of the Rainbow's End from Rosalina, Wilby's grandmother? You've decreed that any picture of the Rainbow's End should be banned from public or private display."

"Let her be, Kilmaz," replied the King. "There has been a long night in our land. The people need to keep hope alive for a new day."

Chapter Three

JOURNEY'S BEGINNING

"It's time for lunch, Wilby," said Lemet. "Let's stop over here." He nosed his horse toward a tree.

Lemet was fifty-five, much older than his horse. Time had furrowed his cheeks, his laugh lines sagged without joy for some time.

"Where will we get the food, Lemet?" Wilby asked. She was tired and stunned by the surprising mission she was pursuing.

"I always carry some provisions," he replied. "Do you like crackers, or biscuits? I have beans, cookies, bric-a-brac, and dried jerky, too."

"I'll try the crackers."

Lemet offered her a small bag of wheat crackers covered with sesame seeds. Wilby took two crackers and munched them slowly.

"Not very tasty, are they?" Lemet frowned. "Sorry, I'm so sorry."

"You don't have to apologize, Lemet. The crackers are fine."

He smiled, and his face brightened. "Well, you're welcome, then."

"How far do we have to go?"

"Well, it's been some time since I've been in these parts of the Kingdom. I'm more often assigned to the eastern edge, where most of the villages are. I've been through the borderlands many times on the water patrol. I have a map. Let me study it." Lemet rose and rummaged in the pack on his horse. He came back with a folded parchment.

"Here we are; it's one of the few remaining maps of Eregon from years ago. I can't remember the last time I used it. I hope it's up to date." He unfolded the parchment and sat down next to Wilby.

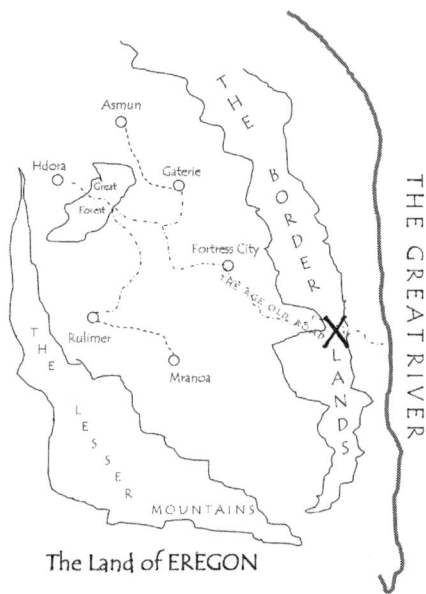

The Land of EREGON

"Look, there's the Fortress City." Wilby pointed to a drawing of the castle on the map.

"That's strange," said Lemet. "The borderlands should be to the right of the Fortress."

"I think you've got the map upside down."

"You're right! So sorry . . ."

"Lemet!"

"Oops. I mean, let me turn it around. That's better. Here, now look at the right edge. Do you see the great plain and then the river?"

"I see them," said Wilby.

"Those are the borderlands. Neer'stazone is past the river. I've never been there."

Wilby studied the paper. "What is this place, marked with the large X?"

"Why, that's where the Rainbow's End was! Sor—I mean, oh my, I didn't realize I still had one of those maps. This was supposed to be turned in, when the new maps were made."

"The Rainbow's End was in *that* place?" asked Wilby. "I've never seen it there. How did it disappear?"

"Oh my. Well, since you are on the mission to bring it back to Eregon, I suppose I can tell you what I know about it. It was many years ago, maybe ten years—has it been that long? At that time, we had a solemn ritual, like a pilgrimage, to go to the Rainbow's End every year to ask for The Almighty's continued blessing on our land. The King and the Seer were the ones who entered the Rainbow's End at daybreak to talk to The Almighty."

"There was a special phrase that the Seer would say." Lemet continued. "Something from a very old scroll. Anyway, there were three men, highly favored in our land, who went with the King and the Seer that year. Rumor has it that when they reached the Rainbow's End, the men pushed the Seer and the King aside and rushed into the Rainbow's End themselves. They had learned the sacred phrase and used it, so the story goes. There was a great storm—an earthquake—and the Rainbow's End disappeared. We never found out what happened to the other men, either."

"Wow! That is quite a story."

"It's a sad story, Wilby." Lemet sighed. "We've lived with trouble since then. Nothing has grown. No green—just enough produce and fruit at the edge of the Great River. We've been able to live on stores of dried food and what comes from the Great River, but even that seems to be running out."

"We were very careful with the water we used in the village," recalled Wilby.

"The Great River on the edge of the borderlands has been our main source of water. When we get there, you'll see how well controlled the access is. The King wants to make sure we don't die of thirst."

The two fell silent for a time. Then they mounted their horses and followed the Age-Old Road toward the borderlands. Dust from the dry earth swirled around them as a breeze blew at their backs. The borderlands were a rocky ridge that ran from north to south as far as the eye could see. The Age-Old Road had been hewn through the ridge many, many years ago.

The road swung back and forth among large rocks and boulders, making many twists and turns.

The borderlands were abandoned. Nothing lived or grew there. Lemet and Wilby rode slowly, passing a large flat area on the right. A great, deep fissure split a wall of rock above the plateau.

"That's the 'X' on the map, Wilby," said Lemet pointing at the fissure. "That's where the Great Waterfall was. The Rainbow rested here. It is so hard to believe that this place was once considered holy ground."

He stopped his horse and looked out over the plateau. A single ray of sunlight, about the same size as Wilby's amulet, fell upon the fissure.

"That sunbeam is all that's left of the sunny skies we used to enjoy here," stated Lemet. "After the Rainbow's End departed, people used to make a pilgrimage here, just to see the light."

"This is the first time I've ever seen it," said Wilby. "Amazing! It's so much brighter than the candle we light at night back home."

"Well, now it's off-limits, Lemet continued. "People have forgotten about it. The Seer says that the sunbeam is a sign that The Almighty still remembers us. Of course, I don't agree."

"Why not?" asked Wilby.

"I think that we've offended The Almighty. Why else would we be punished with such blight? We're under the mark of the cloud, not the Rainbow's End."

They continued their journey for two more days, passing the water brigades coming from the Great River. The King's army led caravans of wagons that carried casks of the clear water into Eregon.

Lemet and Wilby neared the Great River on the third day of their journey. The land at the shore of the Great River was dotted with plants, fruits and vegetables. The sky became brighter, and the gray clouds turned whiter. Wilby scanned the sky above her. At the horizon, yellow shafts of sunlight broke through the clouds, like the rays of a candle pierce the darkness of night.

At that point, the clouds parted, and patches of blue appeared. She stopped her horse and gazed in wonder at the sky. It seemed to have a dividing line: on one side, over Eregon, were dense, gray clouds; on the other side, a sea of blue color spanned the sky. At the very edge in the distance, the bright sun shone overhead.

The Age-Old Road was full of water wagons and many people walking, too. Officers and soldiers of the army patrolled the road and checked the passes of those walking. One officer told them to stop and identify themselves.

Lemet spoke, "I am Lemet, from the King's Royal Guard. I am escorting this young girl, Wilby by name, to view the Great River, by the King's command. We may even take a boat onto the river for a brief time."

"Welcome, Lemet," the officer replied. "I recognize you from your time on the water patrol. Wilby, I'm happy to meet you. We are behind schedule in drawing our water, so I can't offer you much hospitality. We've had a surge of commoners bringing extra containers for their own water. We've increased our efforts to confiscate what goes beyond the weekly limit. We have only one boat, as you know."

"That's fine, officer," Lemet answered. "We will attend to ourselves. It's only a short visit, after all. Where is the boat?"

"It's docked at the water's edge. If you remember, stay away from the middle of the river. It's still not safe; the water barrier allows no one to cross."

"I remember," said Lemet.

The officer moved on. Lemet turned toward a path that led to the water's edge where the boat was waiting. Gray clouds filled the sky over the riverbank.

Wilby followed the clouds to the middle of the Great River. The sky had its border there, with the gray veil of clouds on one side and sunny, blue sky on the other. She had never seen anything like this in her life. Lemet dismounted and signaled Wilby to do the same.

"You're going to have to cross this river, Wilby, to get to Neer'stazone," said Lemet. "I can't go with you, now. I'll distract the others while you leave."

"What do I do?" asked Wilby. "I've never seen a river before, let alone used a boat."

Lemet pointed to two long wooden poles in the boat. "Those are oars. You push them into the water and the boat moves forward. Keep doing that until you reach the other side. Take off your shoes."

Wilby took off her shoes, tied the laces together, and strung them around her neck. She walked into the water toward the side of the boat. She stopped and stood in the water, her legs soaked to her knees.

"This river doesn't hold me up, like the land does!" she gasped.

"Water is not like the land," Lemet said, chuckling. "Be careful. You don't want to go under the water; you won't be able to breathe!"

"How will I get across this Great River? There's no way I can make it!" Wilby's voice trembled with fear.

"There is always a way," replied Lemet. "Get in the boat. Use the oars. Trust in The Almighty to guide you. You'll get across. I have to go now."

Wilby turned toward the boat and waded to its side. The boat rocked back and forth as she tried to climb into it. She pulled herself and some water into the boat on the third try. Lemet untied the rope and pushed the boat from the shore.

"Good-bye, Wilby!" He waved.

Wilby waved back. "Good-bye, Lemet."

She lifted one of the poles and splashed it into the water. The boat moved farther from the shore as the wind picked up. Lemet rode his horse toward the water-drawing station at the Great River's bank. He reached into his saddlebag and pulled out his red cloak, which signified the Royal Guard. He put on the mantle and reined his horse, stopping at the river's edge.

"Hail, there!" he declared. "I came from the King's Fortress, and I must speak to the Officer in Charge."

Geka, the officer Lemet had met on the road, came forward. "Ah, Lemet!" said Geka. "What can I do for you?"

Lemet replied, "We have reports that the water you are supplying to the Kingdom is tainted with a bad taste. Are you contaminating the water when you draw it or put it into the casks?"

"Definitely not!" replied Geka. "We follow the strictest standards of quality, and our men follow the royal procedure."

"When was the last time anyone checked on this?" Lemet demanded. "I think it's time to inspect your operations."

Geka bristled at the suggestion. "Why, that would take every one off patrol! And we have dozens of water wagons that are ready to return to the Kingdom. It would take several hours—all for some talk about a little bad taste?"

"A *little* bad taste?" Lemet answered. "A little bad taste can spoil many appetites and make even the King look bad. Are you willing to risk everyone in Eregon questioning the quality of your work and even riling the King?"

"All right," sighed Geka, "I'll order the inspection."

Lemet replied, "Let me help. I'll watch the road and the riverbank to make sure those who don't belong here don't get in. You get the men to sample each cask on all the wagons and inspect the water-drawing facility."

JOURNEY'S BEGINNING

"Yes, sir!" Geka saluted.

The division of troops began opening the casks and tasting a sample from each one.

In the meantime, Wilby's boat encountered the current of the Great River. The current ran from the shore of Eregon toward the middle of the Great River, not from upstream to downstream as it is with most other rivers.

Wilby pushed the oars into the water to steer the boat. The tailwind behind and the current below pushed the boat along, approaching the middle of the Great River. Wilby neared its center, where the gray clouds met the blue sky above her.

WHOOSH. WHOOSH.

A loud sound of water rising and falling came from the middle of the river. Wilby looked up to see a great wall of water, fifty feet high, which split the river from east to west. The water was like a series of geysers, rising and falling, forming a barrier. White waves and turbulent curls of water surrounded this great wall. The boat began to rock violently, and water spray doused Wilby.

How will I ever get through this? Wilby thought. *I'll die here!* The boat was filling up quickly, and the great wall of water seemed to suck the boat into its middle.

Put on the amulet! The thought occurred to her. *Put on the amulet, now!*

Wilby reached into her sack and pulled out the white amulet that the King had given to her. She slipped it around her neck. The front end of the boat touched the great wall of water, and the wood groaned loudly.

I'm not going to make it! She looked around wildly, hoping for a way to escape.

Another thought pestered her: *Stay in the boat!* Wilby braced herself by holding onto the seat. *Where else can I go?* she thought.

Suddenly, a bright, white light appeared in the middle of the wave, and an arc, like a door, formed in the great wall of water, big enough for Wilby and the boat to pass through. She floated calmly through the arc with the great wall of water surrounding her; it was like going through a tunnel in a mountain.

After several minutes, the water tunnel ended, and Wilby was on the other side of the great wall. The arc and the tunnel of water closed behind her so that there was no more doorway. The sky overhead was blue, and the sun shone brightly. Wilby basked in the warmth of the sunlight, and soon the water that filled the boat and drenched her clothes and shoes was all dried up.

The current on this side of the Great River danced quietly toward the shore of Neer'stazone. Wilby looked ahead at the sandy beach and green trees behind it. The brightness of color and light almost blinded her.

It took several minutes for Wilby's eyes to adjust to this new experience. The boat drifted toward shallow water and landed on a sand bar. "I guess I'm here," Wilby said to herself as she reached for her sack. "I may as well find the Rainbow's End now."

Wilby stepped onto the sand bar and shuffled through the water to the beach. The sand was hot under her feet, and she walked on her heels until she reached a cooler path in the shade of the trees.

Wilby untied the laces of her shoes and put them on. She walked down the path through the trees, which led up a hill and around a bend.

JOURNEY'S BEGINNING

"Where is my granddaughter?" cried Rosalina. "I demand to know!" She had found her way to the King's Fortress and rushed into the Throne Room.

Kilmaz stepped in front of Rosalina. "Come no closer! How dare you enter the King's presence unannounced?"

The King rose from the elegantly carved throne and waved Kilmaz off. "Let her come. She has the right to ask about Wilby."

Kilmaz replied, "As you wish, great King." He returned to his position at the door.

"Where is my granddaughter?" Rosalina asked again.

"She is not here. She is on a mission."

"What kind of mission? Why can't I see her? When will she return? She's only *fourteen* years old!" Rosalina's voice trembled with anger.

"Wilby is on a *great* mission," the King declared. "She is going to return the Rainbow's End to Eregon. You should be honored that Wilby is the one chosen to do this."

Rosalina clenched her fists and snapped in a low voice, "You don't mean to tell me that you've sent her to Neer'stazone! Alone?"

"She has The Almighty with her, and the amulet." The Seer joined the conversation. "She can do this task; it is written in the Scrolls."

"Let me see those Scrolls. I want to see where *Wilby's* name is written. This is the second time someone from your Fortress has seized one of my loved ones to go after the Rainbow's End!" Rosalina broke down in tears. "After Wilby, I don't have anyone left."

"We did not choose the first one, Rosalina," said the Seer softly. "He did things that set all these events into motion. It *is* written in the Scrolls."

"I won't leave the Throne Room until Wilby returns," promised the King. "This throne is my place of prayer. Here I remember Wilby and commend her to the Throne of The Almighty. Here I stay until she returns. You cannot follow her, either."

Rosalina stood silent, her face streaked with tears. "Then I will stay here, too," she said.

"Kilmaz, prepare a room for Rosalina. She will be our guest until Wilby returns."

Chapter Four

In a Strange Land

Meanwhile, Wilby had climbed the hill and walked down the path through the trees past the beach.

Green plants, bushes, and leafy trees grew in abundance along the way. Wilby noticed the even spacing between the plants, bushes, and lush trees as she walked along. The green plants were two feet apart, from side to side and front to back. Each green bush had five green plants around it, and the bushes were spaced five feet apart. All the leafy green trees were twenty-five feet apart and surrounded by five green bushes.

Wilby stopped to look more closely at the green plants. Each plant had exactly five stems; each stem had five leaves. The land around each plant was raked smooth; there were no dead leaves or branches or any type of clutter on the ground.

As Wilby straightened up, she noticed that all the leaves on the plants, bushes, and leafy trees were the same shade of bright, vibrant green. All of the branches and the trunks of the lush trees were the same color brown.

"So this is what green plants, bushes, and leafy trees look like," said Wilby.

As Wilby continued her walk along the path, the amulet on her chest began to hum and vibrate.

Suddenly, a wide, curved, red stripe appeared on the bottom arc of the amulet. Wilby touched it with her right hand. The red stripe felt warm. She paused, wondering what had caused the colored line to appear and what it meant.

Wilby followed the path out of the trees and into a meadow. The green grass was all the same height and the same shade of green.

"I wonder what these colorful things are that are coming out of the ground?" asked Wilby.

"Those are flowers!" a small voice announced from behind her. "Have you never seen flowers before?"

Wilby turned and saw a girl with black hair and green eyes standing in the meadow. She was about four feet tall.

"Well, I saw a picture of flowers once. They were tulips, I believe."

The girl pointed toward the middle of the meadow. "There was a time when there were few flowers in Neer'stazone. Then, some visitors came who showed us how to plant and grow flowers."

The girl joined Wilby near the path. "My name is Umdai."

"How do you do, Umdai? My name is Wilby."

"I am doing well, thank you," replied Umdai.

"Tell me more about the flowers of Neer'stazone," said Wilby.

"Of course! When our visitors came, they carried seeds and spread them around the land, making meadows like this one.

There were all types of flowers then. People would come from the great cities to see the flowers in the meadows. Some meadows had different types and colors of flowers than other meadows. So, the city people would go from one meadow to another hoping to see the different flowers. Some people would pick the rare flowers, so that the meadow was in danger of becoming barren."

"Then what happened?" asked Wilby.

Umdai continued, "The Royal Gardeners Guild was formed to make sure that everyone had a chance to see the same flowers. They didn't want things to be unfair. Some people were afraid that the flowers would spread and take over crops and farmland. So the Royal Gardeners Guild made every gardener take an Oath of Uniformity."

"An Oath of Uniformity? What's that?"

Umdai paused for a moment, "I normally don't talk this much to strangers."

"We could be friends," said Wilby with a smile. "You can talk to a friend, can't you?"

"Friends, oh yes, let's be friends," replied Umdai. "Actually, the Chancellor Masuiah wrote the Oath of Uniformity. After convincing the Governor of the need, the Chancellor decreed that all flowers should be grown in perfect rows, have the same height, the same number of petals, and the same uniform colors. That goes for green plants, bushes, and leafy trees, too."

"Uniform colors?"

"Yes, uniform colors. Actually, we are lucky. Just after the Rainbow's End came, we had a greater variety of colors. My mother still grows flowers of many types and colors in her secret place. But now, throughout Neer'stazone, we have standard hues of the most important colors—red, orange, yellow, green, and blue."

"Those are five colors," said Wilby. "How can five be uniform? And what about purple? Isn't purple a color of the Rainbow's End, too? At least it was on my Gramma's needlepoint."

"You ask such good questions, Wilby!" replied Umdai. "What I mean is that there are five *uniform* colors. There is only one red, one yellow, one green, one blue, and one orange. The Royal Gardeners' Guild has a standard of color engraved on a plaque in the Amudia, the Gate City. Look at your necklace; it has the standard red color."

Wilby's amulet had slipped from beneath her shirt and gleamed in the sunlight. She tucked it back under her shirt.

Umdai continued, "So it is with all that grows here; everything is to be of the uniform color or be uprooted."

"You still haven't said anything about purple," said Wilby.

"We are not allowed to have purple flowers," Umdai sighed.

"Why not?"

"Listen," confided Umdai. "Don't speak so loudly about this color purple. It's not allowed, you know."

"I don't understand." Wilby looked puzzled.

Umdai whispered into Wilby's ear, "There are those who say that purple is the color of The Almighty, and that to have it growing so freely among us would dishonor the Throne of The Almighty. The Chancellor Masuiah has outlawed anything purple, under the punishment of banishment."

"Where would people be banished?" asked Wilby.

"To Eregon! It's such a forsaken place—no colors except brown and black, and I hear that the people there are not fun to be around, either. It's all talk, you know. I've never been there."

"How do you know all these things, Umdai?"

"Our school just finished an entire special lesson about our history. Didn't your school have that lesson?"

"Well, this is the first time I've heard such things," said Wilby. "I'm on my way to tour the land of Neer'stazone. Do you want to come along with me?"

Umdai replied, "I have two sisters and a younger brother at home that I must tend. You're welcome to have dinner with us and stay the night. I live only a short distance from here."

"I would love to stay with you," said Wilby. "You have a family! I grew up alone, just me and Gramma. I wish...," she stopped, then nodded at Umdai. "Thank you for inviting me."

So Umdai and Wilby followed the path through the meadow for the rest of the afternoon.

Around three-thirty, two of Umdai's schoolmates came along. They were dressed in yellow slacks, blouses, and scarves.

"Hey Carol, hey Jacqui," Umdai greeted them.

"Hey Umdai," said Carol. "How do you like our new school uniforms?"

"Pretty bright, huh?" added Jacqui. "We just got them from the village tailor. We're trying them out to wear to school next week."

"Really?" asked Umdai. "Do you think our teacher is serious about wearing uniforms to school? Aren't they more for little kids in the lower grades?"

"Like mom, like daughter!" Carol smiled. "Isn't your mom going to buy you a set of the five new uniforms?"

"Five new uniforms?"

"Yes, five," Jacqui pursed her lips. "You know, one for each of the five uniform colors. Red on Monday, orange on Tuesday, yellow on Wednesday, green on Thursday, and blue on Friday."

"I must have missed that announcement," Umdai said. "By the way, this is my new friend, Wilby."

"Hello, Wilby!" said Carol. "Any friend of Umdai is a friend of ours. Will you be coming to our school, too?"

"No," replied Wilby. "I'm just visiting."

"She comes from a place near the Great River," said Umdai.

"Oh, maybe that area hasn't been told about the uniforms yet," said Jacqui. "Our teacher told us the Chancellor was requiring these new uniforms in all schools by the end of the month."

"I hear the Chancellor has a good looking nephew, about our age," sighed Carol. "I wonder if he's available."

"Me first," said Jacqui. "Umdai, what do you think your mom will say about the new school uniforms?"

"Your mom doesn't like anything uniform, does she?" snickered Carol.

"Leave my mom out of this, please!" Umdai folded her arms.

"Okay, okay, I'm sorry. I apologize. Don't give me that look." Carol took a step back.

"No problem, Carol. Well, we have to get home. Come on, Wilby."

"Nice to meet you, Carol and Jacqui," said Wilby.

"Same here. See you in school tomorrow, Umdai."

Umdai and Wilby continued and arrived at Umdai's home in the village of Vdious.

Umdai invited the neighbor's children to eat with them when they arrived. Wilby recounted her experience of the uniform meadow to Umdai's mother, Kellin.

Kellin smiled while she prepared a simple supper of soup and bread. The supper table was adorned with many colorful flowers.

"These flowers on your table are so different from the ones I saw this afternoon," said Wilby.

"You won't find these flowers in any meadow in Neer'stazone, Wilby," replied Kellin.

"Where do they come from?"

"I'm afraid I can't tell you," Kellin replied. "The flowers come from a secret place. Don't ask questions; just enjoy their fragrance and splendor."

After dinner, they played an exciting game called Pogran, in which each player had to move a small ball through a twisting maze. A player began at the Start area and, if skillful, reached the Finish area to win the game. If a player wasn't careful, the ball would fall into a hole in the maze, and the player would lose.

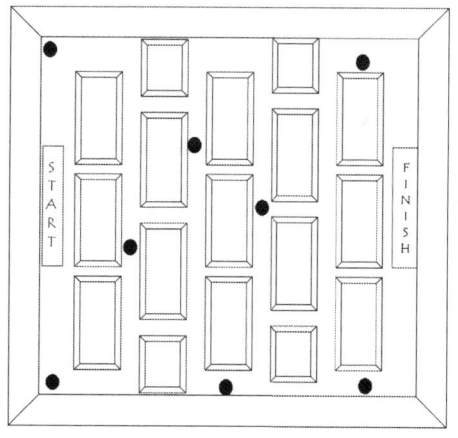

THE GAME OF POGRAN

Turn. Plunk! Drop. Game over.

Twist. Turn. Plunk! Drop. Game over.

It was a new game for Wilby. But she was quick to catch on. She giggled when the ball kept falling into a hole as she wiggled it through the maze.

Her laugh delighted the other children who laughed along with her. After a few attempts and encouragement from Umdai and the other children, she discovered a new move – a wriggle, then a jiggle, now a squiggle. Wilby easily navigated the ball through the maze and reached the finish box.

"Just what is it you are doing?" asked Umdai.

"A wriggle. A jiggle. A squiggle," giggled Wilby. "Let's call it a scriggle!"

"Show me how!" Umdai demanded.

So, Wilby held the Pogran board and guided Umdai through the maze. Then, Umdai showed others.

Everyone imitated Wilby's scriggle that made avoiding the holes and navigating the turns in Pogran so much easier.

"I really enjoyed playing that game," Wilby shared with Umdai as they went to bed. Exhausted from her trip, Wilby fell asleep as soon as she lay down.

The next day, Wilby rose early to say goodbye to Umdai and her family.

"Won't you please stay here with us?" asked Umdai. "Last night was such a wonderful time and the children from next door really like being with you. You showed us how to play Pogran in a whole new way. And enjoy it too!"

"I would love to stay with you, Umdai," said Wilby. "Your friends and family are wonderful! I really wish I had a family and friends like yours. But, I must continue my visit throughout Neer'stazone. You know, you have a new way to play that Pogran game and you can scriggle and giggle like we did last night with your neighbors."

Umdai smiled as she remembered the fun they had playing the game.

"Scriggle Forever!" she giggled.

Wilby took her hand, said goodbye, and departed. Kellin had left before dawn and missed Wilby's departure.

Kellin returned that evening in time to prepare dinner. As they sat down to eat, Umdai started the table conversation.

"Mom, Wilby taught us a new way to play Pogran," said Umdai.

"Oh, what did she teach you?" Kellin replied.

"She showed us how to scriggle."

"She did! What do you do to scriggle when you play Pogran?"

"Well, it's like this," Umdai explained. "When you start the ball rolling, you have to twist and turn the board, so it doesn't drop into the holes. Some times you jiggle. Sometimes you wiggle. When you win, you giggle!"

"Ah, that's precisely how life works here in Neer'stazone. Things don't always work out in a straight path, unlike what the Chancellor Masuiah might say. When I was a young girl, my mother taught me a rhyme to remember:

Dodge and duck

As you twist and turn,

The greatest luck

Comes when you learn."

"What does that mean, Mom?" Umdai was confused.

"Well, learning and thinking for yourself is a precious gift. You don't always succeed on the first try. It's like Pogran. When the ball falls into a hole, you lose the game. But, you have the chance to learn and play again."

"Does that mean I need to keep learning as I get older?" Umdai frowned. "It's hard to learn something new."

"Learning takes time," said Kellin softly. "You can choose whether to learn or not. And you can choose to take the time to learn."

"Do you still learn, Mom?"

"I learn something every day. Especially when I'm gardening. For example, if you listen closely enough, you can hear flowers say 'Ouch!' when their petals are pulled off. It's like they have feelings."

"Mom, what about the five uniform colors?"

"What about them?"

"Well, Wilby didn't seem to know about them. I met Carol and Jacqui on the walk home today. They were wearing their new school yellow uniforms."

"Yellow uniforms? Why yellow?"

"Actually, Mom, they said that we have to wear a different colored uniform, one for each day of the week."

"What? Tell me about it."

"Yes, red uniforms on Mondays, orange on Tuesdays, yellow on Wednesday, green on Thursday, and blue on Friday."

"When was that announced? I didn't hear about it!"

"I didn't either. They said their teacher told them about it. Am I going to get a set of these uniforms, Mom?"

"Let me think about that, Umdai. What else is happening in school?"

"We learned a new rhyme that we have to memorize. It goes like this:

Five fingers and five toes:

Five petals that flowers grow.

Five colors and that's it -

Keeps us all so close-knit."

"Umdai! When did you learn that rhyme?"

"Oh, it was a day or so ago. Our teacher gave us the new rhyme and told us to memorize it. The rhyme came from the Chancellor Masuiah himself."

Kellin frowned. "My dear, there are some things people try to teach you that you have to question. Not everyone has five fingers or five toes. Not every flower has five petals. There are more than just five colors."

"But Mom, all the other kids just went along with the teacher. I don't want to stand out or be made fun of by disagreeing."

"Umdai, I understand. It's hard to stand up for what you know to be true when others say something different. But, you have to be true to yourself, too."

"It's just so confusing, Mom."

"Oh, how I know!" Kellin hugged Umdai and then looked away.

Chapter Five

Making New Friends

Wilby found the Palace Road that led west. For several days, Wilby traveled the Palace Road by foot. She made new friends with the boys and girls who played in the meadows next to the road each day.

She stayed with them in their houses each evening, sharing supper, friendship, and games. They scriggled and giggled as they played Pogran in the new way that Wilby taught them.

Each night, she slept securely in the bed her new friends provided. Each morning, the children asked Wilby to stay with them. Each day, she said the same things that she said to Umdai. Often, she wished she could stay for just one more day. Ah, but she remembered her promise to the King of Eregon to fulfill her mission. Her personal adventure, as Gramma called it.

The next day, as Wilby was walking alone near a large prairie, she heard a soft sound.

Jaaaaa . . . A slight rustle came from the reeds on Wilby's right. *Jaaaa . . . haaa . . . .*

The noise continued, slightly louder. Wilby turned to her right and saw only the reeds swaying slowly. *Jaaaa . . . haaa . . . maaaaaaaaa.* A breeze seemed to whisper in the reeds. *Jaaaa . . . haaa . . . maaaaaaaaa.* It sounded like a breath that was slowly exhaled.

"How strange - Jahaamaa!" Wilby whispered, imitating the breathy sound. She turned her attention back to the Palace Road, and suddenly, a boy appeared, walking toward her. Wilby was startled to see someone else on the road after walking by herself for miles.

"Hello!" she called, suddenly feeling nervous and aware of being alone.

"Hello! Hello!" the boy called back. He was fourteen with blond hair, blue-gray eyes, and a cheerful grin. He stopped about six paces in front of Wilby. "Hello, again!"

"Yes, hello," she replied. "My name is Wilby."

"And I am Jahaamaa. At your service, Wilby!"

"Jahaamaa! What an interesting name. That sounds like something like a breeze might whisper among the reeds."

The boy smiled and shrugged. "Yes, well, that's my name."

Wilby politely changed the subject. "Where does this road lead? You are coming from the direction I am going."

"Oh, this road is the Palace Road. It leads through the city of Nowlingburg and then on to the Palace City, where the Governor lives. Hardly anyone goes this way much. Are you on a grand mission, to go this way?"

"I am touring Neer'stazone. Where do you come from?"

"I am from Amudia, the Gate City. I, too, am touring the eastern edge of the Kingdom. I've seen the Great River and the many meadows that lie between here and the Great River. Now I'm returning home."

"Well, I must be on my way. There are sights to see and things to do."

"Ah, so there are. Are you sure that you wouldn't like a guide? Someone who knows where the Palace Road goes? It's still a long way to the City of Nowlingburg. I've been there many times myself, you know."

"Well, I suppose. Are there places to stay at night along the way?"

"Oh yes! I have lots of friends who can give us a meal and a place to sleep. One of my best friends is Wozner, the son of the Grand Viceroy, Trentum the Great. They live in the city of Nowlingburg. We can visit them on our way there."

"Fine. Let's get started."

And so the two continued toward Nowlingburg. Jahaamaa told Wilby many stories about Neer'stazone, the Palace City, the coming of the Rainbow's End, and the before times. They walked until sunset when they met Jahaamaa's friend Humik, where they stayed overnight.

Every morning their hosts gave them enough food and water for the day. They passed meadows and forests every day, with uniform colors and spacing among the flowers, green plants, bushes, and leafy trees. Each night, Jahaamaa encountered a friend who invited them to supper and provided a place to sleep. On the fifth day, they reached the gates of Nowlingburg.

As they entered the city, Wilby and Jahaamaa strolled down the main street that ran through the city's center. Nowlingburg was laid out like a five-pointed star with different sections of the city on each point: the schools and library on the first point; all the doctors, dentists, and places to make people healthy on the second; the government buildings on the third; and houses on the fourth and fifth points. Down the middle were shops and restaurants, florists, and the flower market in the city's center. Wagons of gardeners lined the main street to bring the flower harvest from the meadows into the market.

As Wilby and Jahaamaa neared the market, a ruddy boy with red hair and freckles called out from the top of a large flower wagon, "Jahaamaa! Look at me!"

"Wozner!" said Jahaamaa. "What are you doing up there? Come here, I want you to meet someone."

Wozner saw Wilby and smiled. He picked two yellow pansies from the pile on the wagon and stepped on the wagon's side.

"Watch this!" he yelled.

Wozner crouched to jump, but his left foot caught on the rope holding the flowers in place as he did so. He fell over the side, startling the horses hitched to the wagon. The horses bolted, pulling the wagon and dragging Wozner along the cobblestone road.

Wilby ran into the street toward the wagon and yelled, "Stop them! Stop them!"

Jahaamaa leaped into the back of the wagon, climbing over the pile of flowers to reach the horses. The wagon plunged forward, heading toward the center of the market amid heavy traffic. Wilby ran beside it, near where Wozner was dangling. She jumped and caught the railing of the wagon; then, she tried to loosen Wozner's foot from the rope.

Suddenly, the horses rounded a corner. A strong blast of wind blew the pile of flowers from the wagon bed, covering Jahaamaa and the horses. Unable to see the road ahead, the horses reared and halted. The wagon stopped instantly.

Wilby freed Wozner's foot from the rope, and he stood up, rumpled and smiling. Wilby felt a vibration from the amulet that she wore under her shirt. An orange stripe appeared above the red stripe. She let go of the railing and bent close to Wozner.

"You saved my life!" Wozner gasped to Wilby. "You *saved* my life!"

"I'm just glad that you're okay," heaved Wilby, out of breath.

"Here, ummm, here are the flowers I wanted to give you. Well, they're a little crumpled. I'll get some other ones."

"These are just fine." Wilby grinned. "Thank you!"

Jahaamaa climbed out of the wagon and joined them. "Wozner! Are you okay? What a ride!"

"I'm okay, really I am. Just a bruise here and there." He turned to Wilby. "My name is Wozner."

"I am Wilby. Nice to meet you."

"Well, Wozner," said Jahaamaa, "it's a twist, of course. Wilby is touring Neer'stazone, and I told her about you and the city of Nowlingburg. On her first visit, she saves your life. Turns and twists, like my uncle says. Don't you think?"

Three soldiers rode up to the spot and surveyed the flower wagon and the pile of flowers on the street as they were speaking.

"Who made this mess?" shouted the soldier with the red armor and shield.

"Captain Frivop, this girl saved my life!" explained Wozner. "The horses bolted and I was being dragged to my death. She risked her life to set me free."

"Hmmph!" snorted Captain Frivop. "Just look at all these flower petals strewn all over the street! You know our ordinance for having things orderly and uniform. Just who is going to clean all this up?"

"I don't believe this! Wozner, the son of the Grand Viceroy, almost died, and all you care about is petals on the street?" Jahaamaa crossed his arms defiantly.

"Hmmph and double hmmph!" Captain Frivop seemed unimpressed by Wilby's heroic action. "I suppose I'll have to file a report."

He waved to the other soldiers, who dismounted and picked up the petals.

"Wilby, Jahaamaa, come to my house," said Wozner. "I have to tell my father how you saved my life today!"

The three teens walked to the Fourth Point of the star-shaped city. Trentum the Great, the Grand Viceroy of Neez'stazone, lived in the largest house of the Fourth Point.

The house was large and contained many rooms of all shapes and sizes. There were typical rooms like bedrooms, baths, a kitchen, and a dining room. Then, the guest rooms were of different shapes, like squares, triangles, and ovals. One room had a spiral staircase and a loft. Others had walls lined with books, mementos, and paperweights of all shapes and sizes.

When the three arrived, Wil and Wes, Wozner's two brothers, were playing in the Blue Triangle room. Wozner's mother, Mrs. Trentum, met Wozner and his friends in the entrance hall.

"Wozner! What happened to you?" asked Lady Trentum in alarm. "Your clothes are rumpled and torn. And you look dirty, too."

"Mother, meet Wilby," Wozner was beaming. "She saved my life today when the horses pulling a flower wagon went berserk. I was being dragged to my death on the street. She stopped the wagon and set me free."

"It was nothing, really, ma'am," blushed Wilby.

"Wozner is right," said Jahaamaa. "I was there and saw what happened. At least, most of what happened."

"Welcome to our home, Wilby," replied Lady Trentum gracefully. "Thank you for saving Wozner's life. You must stay with us as our honored guest."

"I would be honored indeed," said Wilby.

Lady Trentum invited her sons, Jahaamaa, and Wilby into the Grand Parlor, where they played several games together.

When evening came, the Grand Viceroy, Trentum the Great, arrived home from a trip to the Palace City. Wozner and Lady Trentum told him all about Wilby and the flower wagon incident in the market.

At dinner, Viceroy Trentum welcomed Wilby and blessed her for saving Wozner's life. "I am indebted to you, Wilby," he began. "I love my son Wozner very much. He has always had a soft heart."

"Yes, he always wears his heart on his sleeve," teased Wil.

"Heart on the sleeve and giving away flowers on the brain," snickered Wes.

"Boys, I'm speaking to Wilby," replied the Viceroy. "Wilby, I am so glad that Wozner is alive and with us, like all my sons. The Almighty has shown us this favor through you. I want to present you to the Governor for his blessing and reward."

"That is a great honor, Wilby!" exclaimed Wozner. "Not everyone gets to meet the Governor, let alone be honored by him."

"Grand Viceroy Trentum, I am overwhelmed at your generous offer," replied Wilby. "But anyone would have done the same thing to help Wozner, I'm sure."

"No, not everyone would, Wilby," said the Viceroy with a sigh. "There are many citizens who go about their business and ignore helping others when such things happen. People who think of others are rare. That's why it's important to introduce you to the Governor and the other leaders of Neer'stazone. Your example could inspire others. Maybe even the Chancellor Masuiah would learn something."

"The Chancellor is my uncle," whispered Jahaamaa to Wilby. "If there is a banquet, you will meet him there, or maybe when we get to Amudia. He rules over the Court of Uniformity back home."

"Another honor, to be sure," Wilby whispered back.

"Ahem!" Lady Trentum spoke. "It's time for dessert. When you finish, we have family games and our reading hour. Wilby, I'll show you where you can sleep."

The dessert was delicious. Lady Trentum served home-baked almond cookies topped with chocolate sprinkles and a creamy brownie ice cream. Wozner and Jahaamaa devoured a second helping. After dinner, the new friends joined in playing Pogran in the family room.

Wilby giggled as she played, and soon the boys were laughing along, too, at the new way she turned the board at an angle while she played the game. Soon, tired from the events of the day, they went to bed and fell fast asleep.

Chapter Six
At the Governor's Feast

"Wilby! Here is a set of dress clothes and shoes you can wear when we visit the Governor," said Lady Trentum.

Wilby looked up from the book she was reading from the Great Viceroy's library, *The History of Our Land*. "It's beautiful! Where did you get it?"

Lady Trentum held up a pink dress with diamond-like sequins of many colors across the bodice. The skirt was pleated and hemmed with embroidered roses.

"Do you like it? It belonged to my grandmother when she was a young woman. I wore it as a girl on special occasions. We never had a daughter, but I did save it for another special moment, like this one."

"It is *very* beautiful," repeated Wilby with a smile. "If only *my* Gramma could see me dressed like this. . . Thank you for letting me wear it. When are we going to see the Governor?"

"The Grand Viceroy has obtained an audience with the Governor in two days. We leave today to journey to the Palace City. Gather your things so we can pack for this trip."

The Trentum family, Jahaamaa, and Wilby prepared to go to the Palace City. The Grand Viceroy's coach was decorated with the best flower garlands money could buy.

There were five garlands of 125 flowers each – red, orange, yellow, green, and blue. Each petal of each garland was precisely the same size, shape, and color. The Grand Viceroy's attendants stowed all of the luggage and made ready to leave.

"I think your Uncle Masuiah would be very proud of the decorations on the coach," said the Viceroy to Jahaamaa.

"Indeed," replied Jahaamaa. "From what I know of the Code of Uniformity, the flowers on the coach look perfect.

"Yes, they are perfect!" said a man who stood nearby. He was wearing a brown leather hat, which he adjusted on his brow. "I grew them."

"Thank you for making our journey a memorable one," said Lady Trentum.

The party entered the coach, and the man in the brown hat straightened the garlands of flowers so that any wrinkle or twist disappeared. A team of perfectly white horses pulled the carriage down the street.

Wilby looked out the window and asked, "Who is that man?"

"Oh, he's one of the many gardeners in the Kingdom," replied Lady Trentum. "They are so exacting, those gardeners! Everything has to be exactly the same."

"By the decree of the Governor, dear," replied the Grand Viceroy. "He supports the Code of Uniformity and its Court. Jahaamaa, your uncle influences the entire land."

"Yes, he does," said Jahaamaa. "Although, sometimes I'd like a little more variety. It's quite a twist, of course. But don't tell him that. I don't want to get into trouble."

"I know what you mean," Lady Trentum added. "Sometimes I'm afraid that he thinks we people have to be exactly alike, too."

"We don't have to worry, Mother," said Wozner. "We're part of the Grand Viceroy's family. The Governor or anyone else wouldn't make us be different from who we are."

"I was reading about this Code of Uniformity in one of your books, Viceroy Trentum," Wilby said. "The book said that it wasn't always this way. When did things change?"

"I suppose you couldn't remember, could you, Wilby?" asked Trentum the Great. "Things changed about ten or eleven years ago. There was a massive shift in the heavens, and the Rainbow's End came to rest in our land from a distant place. Three visitors came to Neer'stazone at that time; two of them came into power. The third visitor planted many different types of flowers throughout the land in many shapes and colors."

"That was when the Governor established a throne and appointed Viceroys throughout the kingdom. He named his companion, Masuiah, to be the Chancellor. But soon, the meadows with all of the flowers became so popular they were in danger of being raided. To protect the new government, Masuiah wrote the Code of Uniformity and formed the Court of Uniformity to enforce the Code. Then, the Governor established a Royal Guild of Gardeners to ensure the trees, bushes, and flowers would comply."

"Just where are you from, Wilby?" asked Lady Trentum.

"Well, I . . . " Wilby thought hard for a moment. She almost said that she grew up in Eregon; then the King's words echoed in her ears: *Don't tell anyone who you really are.* Finally, Wilby said, "I came from the land by the Great River."

"Ah, the Great River!" exclaimed the Grand Viceroy. "Wilby, do you know where the water comes from that feeds the Great River?"

"No, where does it come from?" asked Wilby. "Does rain fall from the sky and fill the river?"

"No, Wilby," the Great Viceroy explained. "It never rains here; it doesn't have to rain. The Great River is fed by a stream that flows from beyond the Great Mountain. Some say it comes from the Rainbow's End. It may well be, since the stream and the Great River never existed until the Rainbow's End came to rest on our land."

"I see," said Wilby.

"Your parents, Wilby; where are they?" asked Wozner.

"Oh, my parents. My Gramma lives near there, and my father—I don't remember my father or my mother. They weren't there when I grew up. I really wish I had played even one game with them, like we did last night."

"I'm sorry, Wilby," said Jahaamaa. "About your parents, I mean. I didn't know my father or mother, either. I grew up with my uncle, the Chancellor Masuiah. It's quite a twist of life, isn't it?"

"What's quite a twist?"

"Just how our paths have crossed and how all of the things have turned out since then. We are alike in so many ways. It's such a twist, of course."

The travelers grew silent, and the sound of the horse-hoofs clopping on the road fell into a cadence. Everyone but Wilby dozed. She looked out of the carriage at the meadows of red, yellow, orange, green, and blue flowers clapping in the breeze like a vast audience saluting a parade. The horses clopped, clopped, clopped along.

At dusk, the carriage arrived at the gates of the Palace City. A patrol from the Governor's army met them. After recognizing the Great Viceroy, the patrol escorted the carriage to the Palace. The travelers received the best guest rooms on the Palace's outer walls. After a simple supper, Wilby and her companions settled down for a good night's rest.

The visitors dressed in fresh clothes in the morning and toured the Palace City. Like Nowlingburg, the city was laid out like a five-pointed star with different sections of the town on each point: the schools and library on the first point; all the doctors, dentists, and places to make people healthy on the second; the government buildings on the third; and houses on the fourth and fifth points.

Down the middle were shops, restaurants, and florists; in the city's center was the Palace. The main street was lined with banners that read, "Long Live the Governor, our Protector and Friend."

The Palace itself was shaped like a five-point star, each point aligned with a point of the city. The building was exquisite with carved gemstones, inlaid marble, columns of pure gold, and silver spiral steps trimmed with platinum and the rarest of metals.

Garlands of perfect flowers, each with five petals, were carefully draped from balconies and interwoven on the stairway railings. Each point of the Palace held one main window that stretched thirty feet high and fifteen feet wide. Each of the five main win-

AT THE GOVERNOR'S FEAST

dows was made of thousands of pieces of hand-cut glass. The glass of each window was one of the five royal colors: red, orange, yellow, green, or blue.

From a messenger, the chief captain of the Governor's army had learned of Wilby's heroic rescue of Wozner. The captain informed the Governor that Wilby had saved the Great Viceroy's son. The Governor ordered a royal banquet to celebrate the deed. When evening came, the feast began, and dignitaries from across the land joined the celebration.

The Majestic Hall held the banquet. The Hall was shaped like a five-pointed star, aligned with the five points of the Palace. In the middle of the Hall was a five-pointed Throne room with a door on each side. The doors were painted in royal colors: a blue door, a green door, a yellow door, an orange door, and a red door. No one ever entered the Throne Room except the Governor and Chancellor Masuiah.

The guests danced and enjoyed the music; they feasted on vast amounts of every kind of food. The Governor and Governess entered the room, and everyone stood at attention.

"Long live the Governor, our Protector, and Friend," the guests all cried.

The Governor sat under the tall yellow window at the north point of the table. Wilby and the Grand Viceroy were escorted to the Governor, who smiled and spoke to Wilby. She was astounded by the glittering Hall and the array of fine attire worn by the Governor and his wife.

"Now tell me, just how did you save Wozner, son of the Grand Viceroy Trentum? You are just a girl, aren't you? Where did you get the strength to stop the flower wagon so quickly?"

Wilby blushed. "Great Governor, I was helped by a gust of wind. I heard Wozner's cry for help and I ran to the flower wagon, trying to untie him. Just then the horses became startled and sped away, dragging Wozner behind. A great gust of wind rushed upon the flowers, which covered the horses, who stopped running."

"Ah, aided by the breath of The Almighty!" exclaimed the Governor. "Truly, you are a blessed teenager."

"Thank you, Governor." Wilby giggled as she skipped back to her seat at the banquet table near Wozner and his family.

The Governor summoned his palace ministers and whispered to them at length; then, he smiled and dismissed them. After several minutes, the ministers reappeared, carrying a star-shaped box. The Governor stood up and addressed the guests.

"Citizens of Neer'stazone! My friends and favored ones! We gather to celebrate our friendship in a community united by common dreams, laws, and principles. We assemble from the five reaches of the land, under the five banners of color to which we pledge allegiance. Tonight, we honor a visitor, who is also a friend. We honor a person who reached out to help another in need. We honor the valor and swiftness of commitment to the notion of goodwill that we hold so dear. We honor our guest, Wilby, who comes from near the Great River. She saved the life of Wozner, son of our Grand Viceroy Trentum. Wilby, will you please come forward?"

Wilby rose from her place and walked toward the Governor. When she reached his side, he clasped her hand and said, "On behalf of our land, the land of Neer'stazone, I bestow on you the 'Order of Friendship.'"

AT THE GOVERNOR'S FEAST

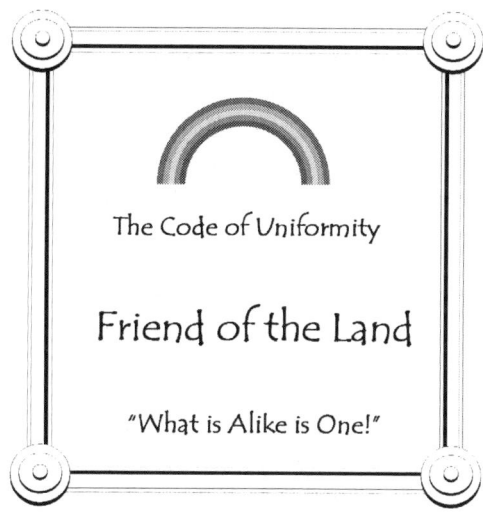

Order of Friendship Award

The Governor handed Wilby a silver plaque with a carved image of the Rainbow's End at the top, adorned in stripes of the five Royal colors. The words "Friend of the Land" were engraved in the middle of the plaque.

The guests applauded as the Governor stepped back and allowed Wilby to speak.

"I am truly grateful for this award," said Wilby with a tear in her eye. "It means so much to me. I feel like I have a new family and that I'm helping. Thank you so much."

She wiped away her tear and made a slight bow. Then she returned to her seat with Wozner and his family. The amulet under Wilby's dress began to vibrate. After several seconds, the vibration stopped.

She excused herself to use the ladies' room. She took out the amulet when she was alone and looked at it. A yellow stripe had appeared on top of the orange and red stripes.

Hmmm. These lines on the amulet are starting to look like the image of the Rainbow's End on the award plaque, she thought.

She returned to their table and sat down.

"Is everything all right, Wilby?" whispered Lady Trentum.

"Yes, I'm fine, I just had to make an adjustment."

"Oh, I see. Yes, having three boys is different than having a daughter."

"I'm fine, really. How do you like the food they're serving us?"

"This is quite a feast, isn't it?" Wozner added. "The Governor really knows how to live. Isn't this hall so amazing? Our teacher has always dreamed of visiting the Palace. Just wait until I get home and I can tell her I saw it first hand."

"Well, we're here because of you - and Wilby," teased Wil. "If you hadn't climbed the flower wagon and got flowers for Wilby, we'd be at home."

"Now, Wil," said the Grand Viceroy. "What did I tell you about teasing Wozner about his soft heart?"

"Sorry, Dad. Sorry, Wozner."

"It's okay, I'm glad to have a soft heart," Wozner smiled. "Just look at all the people you get to meet!"

After the banquet was over, Jahaamaa approached Wilby. "I have to introduce you to my uncle, the Chancellor!" he said excitedly. "Come on, he's right over here."

Chapter Seven

Traveling Through the Countryside

Jahaamaa held out his arm and Wilby took it. He escorted her to the head table where a robust man, impeccably dressed, sat. Jahaamaa cleared his throat.

"Uh humph. Uncle Masuiah, this is Wilby who received the Order of Friendship tonight. Wilby is my friend, too. I was with her when she saved Wozner's life."

"Ahem," replied the Chancellor, "you mean 'Ahem,' Jahaamaa. 'Uh humph' is used by common folks who don't have the right pronunciation."

"Sorry, Uncle. I keep getting that mixed up."

"Never mind, boy," the Chancellor said, flashing a great mouth full of teeth. "So, Wilby. We honor you tonight." He extended his right hand, on which he wore a white glove.

"It's nice to meet you, Chancellor," she answered as she took his hand, which felt rough under the glove.

The Chancellor jerked his hand away quickly. "Do you know the significance of the symbols on the plaque that you just received?" he continued.

"No, your honor. I mean, I think so. Isn't the Rainbow's End a symbol for friendship and well-being?"

The Chancellor laughed like an alligator that bellows before it is about to devour a meal. "Ah yes, a symbol of friendship and well-being. You're quite right. But do you know what that friendship and well-being result from?"

"What do friendship and well-being result from, your honor?" returned Wilby.

"Ah, they result from perfect harmony with The Almighty, which we create in the perfect order of our surroundings. There is rightness in perfect order. The Rainbow's End connects our land, and us, with the Throne of The Almighty, which is beyond sight in the uppermost sky. The Almighty is so far removed from us—who can reach the sky? We have the duty to continue the work of The Almighty in our land. Friendship and well-being are created only when perfect order and harmony exist. We control what we do, and it is by uniformity that we live as one. What is alike is one."

Wilby's eyebrows furrowed. "What you're saying is that we are friends and live in harmony only when we have the same things?"

"No, no, not the same things, the same beliefs. We are to believe the same things, like the truth of harmony and perfect order, and express them in exactly the same way, in each time and place. The Code of Uniformity is our law for making sure that we don't offend The Almighty. The Code shows us exactly how we are to believe. What is *alike* is one."

"I think I understand," said Wilby. "When everything is the same, we are friends of The Almighty."

"Yes. We are also friends of each other. It's a challenge every day to make sure that our thoughts and actions result in this harmony. That's why our colors, our meadows, our flowers, plants, markets, houses, and cities are very much the same. Any variation from these could cause The Almighty to be displeased with us, and that would be a disaster. The Kingdom is blessed to have people who uphold the Code of Uniformity through the example of their work. Take the gardener, Bilnot, for example. For ten years straight, he has won the Uniformity Award for the way he tends his meadows. A man of real integrity and mission, that Bilnot."

"This Bilnot fellow seems so very interesting. I think I saw him arranging the flower garlands on the Great Viceroy's coach just before we came here. He was wearing a brown leather hat."

"That's Bilnot, all right," replied the Chancellor. "He's made so much progress in creating uniformity in this land!"

Lady Trentum strolled up to Masuiah and took his arm. "Oh, Chancellor, Wilby is such so young. She has plenty of time to learn about such deep things. I think it's time for us to return home before it gets too late."

"Lady Trentum, it is never too early to teach our teens about the reasons for our ways of life," replied the Chancellor. "If they stray from our traditions while they are teens, it will be too late when they become grown-ups."

"You are as witty as you are charming, Chancellor. Perhaps Wilby will visit Amudia someday, and you'll have the time to continue your discussion."

"It would be my pleasure, Lady Trentum," responded the Chancellor. "Good evening."

"Good-bye, Chancellor," said Wilby.

Wilby and the Trentum family retired to their room in the Palace for the night. Wilby admired the plaque for several minutes, reflecting on her mission to return the Rainbow's End. Then, she put the award away in her sack. The following day, they returned to the city of Nowlingburg. Jahaamaa went back home to Amudia with his uncle Masuiah.

Wilby had stayed with the Trentum family in Nowlingburg for two weeks after the banquet with the Governor. Then she said, "It's time for me to continue my journey through Neer'stazone."

"Where will you go now, Wilby?" asked Lady Trentum. "Why don't you stay here with us? You've become like part of our family. We'd love to have you live with us."

"Oh, you have been such a wonderful family to me," replied Wilby. "I really wish that I could stay."

"Well, then. It's settled. You can stay as part of our family."

"I can't. You have been so kind and I couldn't ask for anyone better to stay with, but I must see the Great Mountain."

"The Great Mountain is a very long way, Wilby," interrupted the Grand Viceroy, who stood in the doorway to the room. "It borders Amudia."

"I still must go there, just to see it," replied Wilby. "Amudia? Don't Jahaamaa and the Chancellor live there?"

"Yes, they do. Amudia is the Gate City—the perfect model of all cities in Neer'stazone—although I wouldn't want to live there. But no matter, I have business in a small village near there soon, and I can take you as far as Bilnot's meadows just outside of the city."

TRAVELING THROUGH THE COUNTRYSIDE 63

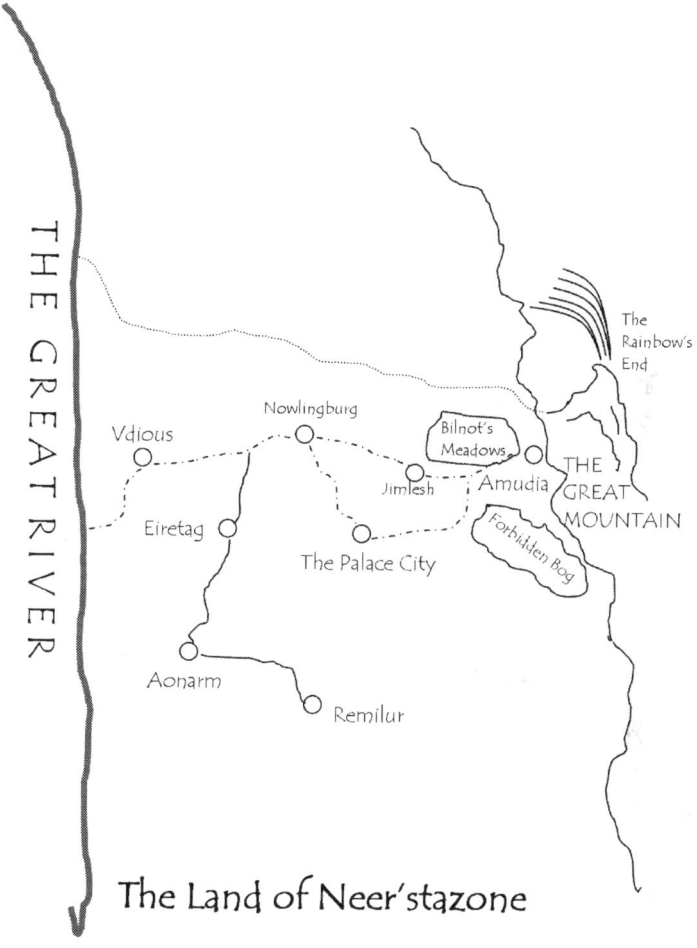

The Land of Neer'stazone

"Bilnot's meadows?" said Wilby. "Is that the Bilnot the Chancellor talked about at the banquet?"

"It's the same one, Wilby," Mrs. Trentum replied. "He always wears a brown leather hat. Do watch out for him, though."

"Why should I watch out for him? Is he dangerous?"

Lady Trentum began to answer but stopped, bit her lip, and said nothing. The Grand Viceroy made ready for the trip, and after a tearful hug with Wozner and Mrs. Trentum, they set out the next day. They took the same route to the Palace City but detoured around it. As the journey continued, they began to discuss the latest events.

"Have you been in this part of Neer'stazone before, Wilby?" asked the Grand Viceroy?

"No, I haven't," replied Wilby. "What is unique or different about this area?"

"Oh, it's much the same as the rest of the land. Many meadows along this road. There are two roads into Amudia. This road goes through Jimlesh, which joins the road from the Palace City. When the Chancellor visits the Governor, he goes directly to the Palace City. You met both of them at the banquet held in your honor. What do you think of them?"

"Well, uh, um, I don't know what to say. They're different, but they seem alike too."

"I think you're catching on, Wilby," replied the Grand Viceroy. "At first glance, they may appear the same. Just remember, things aren't always the same beneath the surface if you know what I mean."

"I think I understand. The Chancellor really is determined to make appearances the same."

"Correct! Appearances can be deceiving. Just be on your guard when you get to Amudia."

After four more days, they reached the town of Jimlesh, where the Grand Viceroy was to visit.

"Amudia is only a day's walk from here," said Trentum. "Just follow the main road and it will lead you directly to the city."

Wilby grasped the Grand Viceroy's arm and touched her forehead to his hand. She thanked him and said goodbye. Then, she walked out of town on the main road toward Amudia.

After two hours, she sat down near the side of the road to rest. She was tired from all of the events in the past weeks and missed being home with Gramma. Soon, three figures came by on their way to Amudia. They stopped to talk with Wilby.

"Hello, there!" said Marbo, a tall, thin man merrily. "We are marching to Amudia. We are pilgrims on our way to see the Rainbow's End at the Great Mountain!"

Wilby straightened up. "You are going to see the Rainbow's End?"

"Oh yes!" replied Jiana, a short, round woman. "We've never seen it before, but everyone tells us it is a sight to behold. It's right behind the Great Mountain."

"Of course, no one can get very close to it," said Rogzy, the third pilgrim. "There are patrols all around the base of the Great Mountain. The Chancellor wants to protect the Rainbow's End as a national treasure."

"Well, you've heard the legends about Eregon, haven't you?" said Marbo. "The Rainbow's End used to be there, they say. But someone tried to steal the End and turned the entire land into a desert."

"Oh, yes!!" cackled Jiana. "That's so much like the people of Eregon. What a foolish lot!"

"Have you ever been to Eregon?" asked Wilby.

"The Almighty forbid that!" exclaimed Rogzy. "There's a Great River to protect us from any invasion from Eregon."

"The Chancellor has called the people from Eregon our arch-enemies," added Marbo. "He is so brave to intercede with

The Almighty for all of us in Neer'stazone. Why, what would happen if we had no Rainbow's End here? It would be chaos!"

"Glory to Masuiah!" said the Rogzy. "He has been a savior to us. He's created the Code of Uniformity, built Amudia, and maintained the prize meadows, too. We are so fortunate to visit his city and make a pilgrimage to the Great Mountain. I hope we are on the right road."

"This road is the only way to Amudia," replied Jiana. "Lots of people walk this way, I've heard."

"I've been walking this road for two hours, and you are the first ones I've seen today," said Wilby.

"Oh, this must be the early season," responded Rogzy. "Most people come in the summer. Anyway, we're so excited to be on our way."

"Not only that," continued Marbo, "we'll get to see the prize meadows of Bilnot—the best in Amudia. And they are so close!"

"Yes, this will be a pilgrimage to remember!" exclaimed Jiana. "Goodbye!"

"Goodbye," Wilby waved.

She remained sitting as the three pilgrims shrunk from sight. The day was pleasant—sunny and warm. A slight breeze brushed through her hair. She felt a thumping vibration from the amulet she wore. She pulled the amulet from under her clothes, and a green stripe had appeared.

The green stripe arched over the yellow, orange, and red stripes. *Hmmm. This is so strange,* she thought.

After ten minutes, she rose and continued her walk. She walked another two hours and came to a crossroads. At the junction stood the gardener who wore the brown leather hat.

"Good day!" said Wilby.

"I suppose it's good," said the gardener, scowling. He pulled down the brim of his hat.

"Haven't I seen you before?" asked Wilby. "Weren't you in the city of Nowlingburg, decorating the Great Viceroy's carriage for his trip to the Palace City?"

"You may have seen me there; I often check on the flower market," replied the gardener. "These flowers aren't quite right, though."

"What is wrong with the flowers? They look beautiful to me. My name is Wilby."

The gardener pointed to a patch of flowers growing next to the road. "I don't have time to greet or recognize you. Look, the flowers on that side of the road have five petals, but the ones on this side are not right. Some have six petals or even eight, but not five. What we need is order. I have to make these right."

Wilby asked, "Do the flowers want to be made all the same? Don't they have a say in this?"

"That's very nervy of you to question how I treat these flowers!" the gardener retorted. "This land was assigned to me. **I** am the gardener. In fact, I am a leading member of the Guild. I planted the flowers when I came here, so now they're mine. Flowers don't have feelings; why should they care? They just grow. Besides, your medallion is turned upside down!"

"My medallion is turned upside down?" Wilby looked puzzled. As she had bent down to examine the five-petal flowers, her amulet had slipped out.

"Yes, twisted! Look at it, how the colors are arranged—green on top of yellow, orange, and red. Anyone can see that's how the land looks at sunset. Except the green should be on the bottom, and the red on top. Would you please put it in the right order? Now stand aside, I have work to do."

The gardener reached into his holster and pulled out his gardening shears. He began to snip the sixth, seventh, and eighth petals from the flowers so that now there were only flowers with five petals, like the ones across the road.

For all his bluster, he went about it rather gently, not wishing to step on the flowers or bend their stems; after all, the land was only assigned to him. Soon, the entire patch was done, full of five-petal flowers. The meadow was just like the one across the road. The extra petals were lying on the dirt.

"Now look at this!" The gardener frowned. "The flowers are right, but these extra petals won't do. They're messing up my prized meadow!"

"What will you do now?"

"Hmmm. Let me think." The gardener pushed up the brim of his hat. "I can pick up the extra petals from the dirt right now or just let the wind blow them away."

"Some say there is wisdom in the wind," Wilby stated.

"Wisdom? In the wind? I don't believe it. I never know when the wind will come if it comes at all. I don't like trusting the wind, you know. Sometimes it comes; sometimes it doesn't. And you can never tell how hard it will blow. It may be some time before a wind comes that is strong enough to blow these petals away. I hate to leave my prized meadow looking untidy and out-of-order. I have awards to win. Who knows when the awards committee will visit? Say, you're not one of them, are you?"

"One of whom?"

"One of those sneaky judges who travel the land making sure that everything is uniform."

"No, I'm not," said Wilby.

"That's good," said the gardener. "I guess I'll just have to pick up the petals now."

And so the gardener bent over and scowled as he pulled down the brim of his hat. He picked up the extra petals that were lying on the dirt. Soon, the patch was clean, and the five-petal flowers were arranged in neat rows. The gardener stood up; his hands were full of flower petals.

"I guess I'll move on," said Wilby. "Have a good day."

"I suppose it might get better now," complained the gardener. "Once I figure out where to put all these petals!"

Wilby turned left at the junction. She had walked only five steps when a strong gust of wind rose rather sharply. A shower of dozens of flower petals fluttered past. The road stretched ahead of her toward Amudia, the Gate City with the Great Mountain and the shining Rainbow's End.

Chapter Eight

SECRETS TO KEEP

"Wisdom in the wind! Can you imagine that? And then, a gust came along and blew the flower petals out of my hands and across the road." Bilnot recounted the episode with Wilby to his friend, Kellin.

"Why are you surprised, Bilnot?" asked Kellin. "Remember, life is strange with its twists and turns. Just who do you think this Wilby is?"

"I don't know where she's from. I've never seen her in these parts before. Her use of words was strange, although she seemed like a normal teen to me. The only thing that was distinctive about her was a round medallion she wore that had a twisted image of the land."

"What does a twisted image of the land look like?"

"The colors were upside down—red under yellow under green. It was like sunrise turned upside down."

"Very odd. Let's change the subject, Bilnot. What do you think about the Guild's report that the Governor is looking for a new Royal Gardener?"

"I don't understand it. What happened to the last one?"

"You mean the last ones. There have been four Royal Gardeners in the last year. The Governor just doesn't seem to be satisfied with their results."

"What is he looking for? A miracle worker?"

"The word is that the Chancellor is pushing him to have even more uniformity in the Royal Gardens. This goes beyond the usual five-petal blossoms like we learned when we were apprentices at the Gardeners Guild."

Bilnot thought hard. "We really were taught that five-petal blossoms were the preferred blossom, weren't we? Since then, I've never thought it should be any other way. Have you?"

Kellin leaned closer and whispered, "Actually, I have a secret plot where I have been experimenting with other sizes and shapes of flowers for some time now. Each one is different."

Bilnot gasped. "You've done what?!! Do you know what the Chancellor would say if he learned what you're doing?"

"Come on, Bilnot! When are you going to let go of that teaching? You've never seen a fourteen-petal rose, a dozen-petal chrysanthemum, or a blue astiff, have you?"

"Well, not that I recall. I don't know what I'd do if I did see one of them. I'm so quick to make sure that five-petal flowers thrive, I used to snip the petals from six and eight-petal ones."

Kellin frowned, "Do you mean to tell me that you still believe that all shapes and sizes of flowers are to look the same?"

"That's what the Chancellor teaches, Kellin. Fortunately, I found a five-petal flower that I can plant where I don't have to do any snipping. A pansy. And, with the greatest luck, I learned that pansies grow so thick and so quickly."

Bilnot shook his head, pondering Kellin's defiant attitude. "That girl, Wilby, said something else that was strange. When I told her that all the flowers must have five petals, she asked me how the flowers felt about it. Can you believe anyone who imagines that flowers have feelings?"

Kellin was silent.

Bilnot continued, "I haven't thought that anything other than a five-petal flower could have its own beauty. There has been such order to a field of five-petal flowers standing at attention. I've won the district award from Chancellor Masuiah for ten years in a row, you know. The people of Neer'stazone look up to me. They like to visit my prize meadows. If you're so interested in seeing variety grow, why don't you apply for Royal Gardener? Maybe *you* could change the Governor's mind."

"Bilnot, you *know* why," whispered Kellin. "I am the only woman gardener left in the Guild. There were many women who had been gardeners, before the time of the Governor, Masuiah, and their Code of Uniformity. They grew many shades, shapes, and varieties of flowers. After the Code was instituted, any gardener who didn't comply was forced to pick petals and make floral arrangements. Besides, I love variety. Anyone who becomes the Royal Gardener must practice uniformity."

Bilnot stretched his neck and pulled at his collar. He was getting uncomfortable with the conversation.

"Bilnot, aren't you tired of the same old thing?" Kellin continued. "Aren't you bored with the same routine? The same colors? The same flowers? The same shape? The same size? Will you come to see my secret plot? I want you to see how the different flowers blend with each other. It's a special type of beauty."

"I'd like to see what you're growing, Kellin. But I don't want anyone to see me there. I have it! I'll wear a disguise. That way, word won't get back to the Chancellor. When should we go?"

Kellin replied, "The day after tomorrow. I'm harvesting tomorrow, but I'm free the day after. Let's meet at the road's junction that leads to Amudia, say about six-thirty in the morning. You have to see the sunrise on the dew to appreciate the fullness of the plot. Make sure to bring a large sack with you."

"Six-thirty at the junction, the day after tomorrow it is. Farewell, Kellin."

The dawn came quickly, streaking the sky with red, orange, and yellow light.

Kellin was not at the junction when Bilnot arrived. He was dressed in his best clothes, which he wore once every three years. That was his disguise.

There were fresh footprints and hoofprints in the dirt at the junction, like a large troop passed through. Bilnot stood impatiently, shifting from one foot to the other.

A slight breeze rustled through the knee-high reeds on the east side of the road. Bilnot looked in that direction and noticed two white papers stuck on a stem. He carefully poked among the reeds and retrieved the papers.

One of them was a note from Kellin.

Dear Bilnot,

I'm sorry that I can't be with you this morning. An emergency came up. I've drawn a map to my secret plot. Still, think that there are only five royal colors? Wait until you see this garden. I call it my "Hope Patch." Get there before the sun has fully risen. Stay there as long as you like, but destroy the map before leaving. I'll talk with you soon to learn about your experience.

Kellin.

Bilnot glanced at the map. The hidden plot was very close to the junction. In fact, it was only a ten-minute walk past the Forbidden Bog. *The Forbidden Bog! No one goes there. It's off-limits, like the Rainbow's End. Why in the world would Kellin garden in that forsaken place?*

Bilnot found the path that led past the twisted oak tree and the fallen pine. The mist on the bog seemed to reflect the early morning sky. Bilnot looked carefully and skirted the water's edge. *At least it's serene here,* he thought.

After fifteen minutes, he came to a clearing. The sun just cleared the horizon, lighting up a field of bright colors that seemed to dance in the breeze.

Azure astiphs, yellow marints, coral blukas, and pink fourteen-petal roses were here. There were flowers of many sizes and shapes that Bilnot did not recognize. There were *hundreds* of different hues of color. The rows of flowers twisted and turned throughout the garden – they were not orderly or evenly spaced.

Awestruck, Bilnot wandered toward the middle of Hope Patch. When he reached the center, he stopped in his tracks.

In front of him were giant dark-purple tulips, three feet high, growing amid a clump of red pansies. Yet, the petals of the purple tulips were unlike any other tulip. Instead of folding into the shape of a cup, these petals stood fully stretched out into a circle.

"This is incredible!" Bilnot shouted. "Have I ever seen anything like this before? Somehow, it seems familiar to me."

He continued to wade through the field, taking in all the fragrances and colors. His best clothes became stained with the thick mud, but he took no notice.

A row of ten-foot-high yellow-blue uvas waved merrily back and forth. *Kellin is a genius!* Suddenly, something woke up in Bilnot's mind that had been asleep for nearly ten years and his heart felt soft again. He remembered why these flowers seemed familiar. "I feel so dazed. It's like Eregon was—so many years ago!"

A wall of fifteen-foot-high sunflowers beckoned in the breeze. "Sunflowers!" He smiled for the first time in a decade. "There must be sixty petals on each one. Peace flowers, too! They are like the sunlight planted in the ground."

Bilnot spent the rest of the morning touching and sniffing the multitude of flowers in the hidden patch. *There's something I must do*, he thought.

He took the large sack and harvested flower seeds and the dark-purple tulip bulbs. When his pack was full, he staggered back to the junction, overcome by the richness he had just witnessed.

Amudia is called the Gate City because of its five massive colored gates. Like the Palace City, Amudia was shaped like a star.

A towering wall surrounded the city; there was a different gate at each point of the star. Entering through the Blue Gate led to the residential section of the city. The Green Gate led directly to the city market. The Yellow Gate was the entrance to the school and city archives. The Orange Gate opened to the commercial district.

The Red Gate opened onto a promenade that led to the city hall and temple with the Court of Uniformity.

Amudia stood at the edge of the Great Mountain. The Great Mountain itself rose through the clouds, and the Rainbow's End rested at the top on the west side. The walls at the base of the Great Mountain were sheer rock for hundreds of feet, except for one spot.

In the city wall, between the Blue and Red Gates, was a small purple door that could hardly be called a gate; it looked as thin as a needle's opening compared to the other Gates. On the other side of the purple door was a pathway that led through the foothills of the Great Mountain and up toward its summit.

The Chancellor Masuiah was the only one in the land who could enter through the purple door. He did this at regular times when he wasn't traveling.

This day, Masuiah left the chambers of the Court of Uniformity and slipped away down a narrow hallway toward the purple door. He removed a purple amulet rimmed in white, worn around his neck. He inserted the amulet into a slot in the door. The door swung open toward the Great Mountain. After Masuiah passed through, the door closed behind him.

Masuiah walked up a flight of six stone steps, each with a different color of the Rainbow's End—red, orange, yellow, green, blue, and purple. As he knelt on the purple step, he opened a small purple crystal box and retrieved a ragged fragment of an ancient parchment scroll.

Masuiah unfolded the fragment and read the words aloud, *"What is alike is one. How good it is. What is one is good and pleasing to The Almighty."*

He closed his eyes to meditate on the Scroll's message. After several minutes, he rose with a deep sigh of satisfaction, folded the parchment, and put it back into the crystal box. He walked down the steps, opened the purple door, and returned to the Court's chambers.

Meanwhile, Wilby walked down the Grand Road to Amudia. As she neared the Gate City, the forest shading the road gave way to one meadow after another. Each meadow was meticulously arranged; each was set in concentric circles of blue, green, yellow, orange, and red flowers. Wilby was sure that each flower had only five petals.

A contingent from the Uniformity Patrol watched each meadow to protect it from being raided by overeager citizens. Wilby knew she was nearing the end of her journey. She walked faster, eager to reach the Gate City.

Wilby entered Amudia through the Orange Gate. She walked along the streets, noting the perfect arrangement of the stones that made up the buildings and shops of the Commercial district. As she neared the city center, she heard a familiar voice.

"Hi, Wilby! I'm glad to see you." It was Jahaamaa.

"Hi, Jahaamaa," Wilby grinned, delighted to see her friend. "What are you doing here?"

"I live here, Wilby, with my uncle, Chancellor Masuiah. Remember? Welcome to Amudia!"

"Thank you! This is my first time visiting Amudia. Could you show me around?"

"I would be happy to show you anything that you would like to see. Where would you like to start?"

"Why not start right here? "Although, I have heard so much about the Great Mountain. I would like to visit that place, too!"

"No one can visit the Great Mountain," Jahaamaa frowned as he explained, "Only my uncle can go there. But I'll show you how he gets there."

"Okay. Where are we now?"

"We are in the Commercial District. Amudia has five districts. This is where we shop and buy services for our homes. Look, there's Briggser's Bakery. They make the best cookies in Amudia. Or there, that large building on the corner, that's Lornam's shoe store; they have the best tennies in town."

Jahaamaa continued to point out the best and unique shops that citizens and tourists could visit. They moved along and came to the marketplace. There were dozens of flower carts gaily arrayed with garlands of five-petal flowers.

Crowds of people surrounded the flower carts, for it was Saturday, the day when fresh flowers had been brought from the meadows. There was a commotion among the people near the flower carts. A woman had turned over several carts, spilling their flower garlands all over the street.

Jahaamaa turned to Wilby and whispered, "There she goes again."

The woman spoke loudly to all of the citizens who gathered there. "People of Amudia do not be deceived! These flower garlands are trickery! The flowers in them are not what is grown in the meadows. Not every flower has five petals."

"Who are you?" cried one of the cart owners. "What are you talking about?"

"I am Kellin, of the Royal Guild of Gardeners. I know what is in the meadows—flowers that are made to look alike. There are scores of men and women who pluck petals from flowers to make them appear as if all flowers have five petals. There are more than the five uniform colors, too."

She turned and picked up a flower garland and held it above her head. "Is this what you want to decorate your homes, your places of business? The beauty of creation arranged always the same? Are we to be all alike, too?"

"I've seen her somewhere before," whispered Wilby. "I know! Many days ago, I stayed at her home."

"Watch out for her," Jahaamaa mumbled. "She's not in very high favor with my uncle. She is always finding fault with the Code of Uniformity."

Kellin stopped her speech and looked in their direction. She smiled as her eyes caught Wilby's.

"Come on!" Jahaamaa tugged at Wilby's arm. "Let's go."

Several horses raced toward the overturned carts as Wilby and Jahaamaa left the market. A squad of Uniformity Police dismounted and surveyed the area.

"Arrest her! She's gone too far!" said the leader. The men seized Kellin and took her away to await a hearing at the Court of Uniformity.

Chapter Nine

Entering the Purple Door

Jahaamaa took Wilby through the residential district to his uncle's house. They ate a simple lunch of sandwiches and lemonade. "You must be tired from your journey, Wilby," Jahaamaa said. "Would you like to rest now?"

"Actually, I feel refreshed by the lunch. You promised to show me the Great Mountain. May I see that now?" Wilby winked at him.

"Well, I can't show you the actual mountain. I'm afraid that the Chancellor would object. But, I tell you what; let's go to the Court of Uniformity. The entrance is there and I can show you that. No one is supposed to go near it, but after all, you belong to the Order of Friendship, you know."

Jahaamaa led Wilby to the center of the city. He avoided going past the marketplace, detouring around the library and city archives. They arrived at the Court of Uniformity and went inside. There were many hallways and chambers surrounding the main courtroom. They walked around the main courtroom and passed down a narrow corridor behind it. Jahaamaa stopped in front of the purple door.

"This is it, I think," he said. "This is the purple door that my uncle enters to go to the Great Mountain."

"Can we open it and just take a look?" asked Wilby. "I learned that pilgrims come to the city, just to see the mountain from the courtyard."

"I can't open it. There is no door handle. There is only this slot," Jahaamaa pointed to a disc-shaped slot on the right side of the purple door. "My uncle has the only key. Actually, it's an amulet that he wears under his shirt. I've heard him say that he comes here to pray and say a sacred phrase whenever there is a case to be tried in Court."

Wilby asked, "Do you know what that phrase is?"

"Not all of it. There's something about pleasing The Almighty, and when everything is alike we are one. That's not exactly it, but something like it."

"Is everything alike?" asked Wilby. "Look at you and me. Are we alike? You're a boy and I'm a girl."

"Well, my uncle says that's why we have our Code of Uniformity, to please The Almighty. This door is the only place in all of Neer'stazone where purple is allowed."

"Why is that?" asked Wilby.

"I think it's because the Rainbow's End is here. There's a story about purple being the top color of the Rainbow's End that touches the sky, closest to The Almighty. So it's not right to have that color here on earth."

As they stood there, the purple door creaked open. The Chancellor came through the door and stopped in surprise when he saw them standing in the hallway.

"Jahaamaa! What are you doing here? And who is this girl?"

"Hi, uncle!" Jahaamaa squealed. "I'm giving my friend, Wilby, a tour of Amudia. She heard about the Great Mountain. I told her that she couldn't see it, but that I would show her the purple door. You remember Wilby, don't you? You were there at the Palace when she was awarded the Order of Friendship by the Governor, you know."

"Wilby, ah yes," replied the Chancellor. "Jahaamaa! Jahaamaa! What were you thinking? This door is not on the official tour list for visitors. Very few citizens of Amudia have ever been here, either."

"Well, while we're here with the door open, can we at least look at the Great Mountain?" asked Wilby.

The Chancellor gave a half-frown. "Well...., okay, why not? I suppose there's no harm in looking. Go ahead, but be quick about it."

Wilby and Jahaamaa poked their heads through the purple door and gazed at the Great Mountain. The top was covered with clouds, the only place in Neer'stazone where clouds gathered. The Rainbow's End glistened beyond the clouds at the mountain's top.

"It's very beautiful!" exclaimed Wilby. "Thank you for letting me see this."

The Chancellor pointed toward the top step of the colored stones, "Do you see that small altar? That's where I beseech the wisdom of The Almighty whenever I must judge a case in the Court of Uniformity. In fact, that's what I was just doing. We have a hearing about the gardener Kellin in Court today. As my guest, would you like to see what happens at a hearing, Wilby?"

"Why, I-I-uh-all right," Wilby stuttered. She wasn't sure she wanted to listen to a hearing. Hearings and trials don't often have happy endings, but how could she say no to the Chancellor?

"Good!" exclaimed the Chancellor as he slammed the purple door shut. "Jahaamaa, please guide our guest to the main courtroom. I will meet you there."

Jahaamaa and Wilby took seats near the back of the visitor's section in the courtroom. "Don't you think that it's a twist that we're sitting here," whispered Jahaamaa to Wilby, "after all we witnessed today?"

"Yes, it's very much a twist," she answered. "Like I told you, I've met Kellin before and even stayed at her house. I don't think she did anything wrong. Do you?"

"Of course she did!" mumbled Jahaamaa. "Now, don't *you* get involved. You're only a guest here."

The Court came into session, and the Chancellor took his place behind the judgment bench.

"What is this hearing about?" he asked the prosecutor.

"Your honor, Chancellor Masuiah," said the prosecutor, "we have arrested a member of the Gardener's Guild, a woman named Kellin, for disturbing the peace in the marketplace. She overturned flower carts and publicly challenged the Code of Uniformity. She called our meadows, flowers, and garlands a fraud." He pointed to Kellin, who stood at the defense table.

Masuiah stared at Kellin for a long time. She stood tall and stared back defiantly.

"What is alike is one," he said. "It has been a very long time since anyone dared to openly challenge the Code of Uniformity.

It forms the basis of our law. The meadows are the basis of our economy. Detain her. I must consult the Governor about this case." With that, he rose and left the courtroom.

The court guard led Kellin away past the place where Wilby and Jahaamaa sat. "Wait!" she said. "Those two were in the marketplace today when this happened. I want them to be my witnesses!"

The guard stopped. "Will you be my witnesses?" Kellin pleaded with Jahaamaa and Wilby.

"I-I can't." stated Jahaamaa. "I'm related to the Chancellor."

Kellin turned to Wilby. "You look so familiar. How about you?"

"Don't get involved!" Jahaamaa hissed at Wilby.

"Well, really–I'm just visiting," said Wilby, "but I would like to talk with you before I leave. Are you allowed to have visitors?"

The guard interrupted, "The accused may have only one visitor until the case is brought to trial."

"I choose her to be my visitor," said Kellin. "Can you come this evening?"

"Why, y-yes," replied Wilby. "I will come."

"The accused will be held in a small cell near the back of the Court," interjected the guard. "Come to the main entrance before ten o'clock." Then he led Kellin away.

"Just what do you think you're *doing*?" demanded Jahaamaa. "She's *trouble*, I tell you! My uncle will be furious that you are visiting her."

"It is a kind thing to do, Jahaamaa," replied Wilby. "She was kind to me when I stayed at her house. She has a daughter my age. She lives very far away and probably needs a little company. Will it hurt to play a simple game, like she would do with her daughter, and give her a little company?"

"Well, I guess not," muttered Jahaamaa. "I'll have to sneak you out of the house, though. Visitors are not allowed on the streets after nine-thirty without a citizen accompanying them."

They left the Court of Uniformity and toured the rest of the city before returning to Jahaamaa's house to eat a light supper. Wilby and Jahaamaa played a few games of Pogran together. She had Jahaamaa laughing so hard at her funny jokes and novel way of playing that his sides hurt.

Just before nine-thirty, Wilby picked the game of Pogran to take with her on her visit to Kellin. Then, they returned to the Court. A guard led Wilby to a small room where she waited for Kellin to arrive, while Jahaamaa remained behind. Shortly, Kellin came and sat with Wilby at the table. The guard left and closed the door.

"It is good to see you again," said Kellin. "Your name is Wilby?"

"Yes. You remember me," replied Wilby. She spread the Pogran game on the table.

"I remember the day when Umdai brought you home for dinner. Now, we're meeting here." Kellin lowered her voice. "You're not from Neer'stazone, are you?"

Wilby looked around the room to make sure they were alone. "No, I'm not," Wilby whispered. "How did you know?"

Kellin smiled. "When you first visited my house, Umdai told me that you asked many questions about the flowers. Everyone from Neer'stazone knows the answers to those questions. Parents must teach them to their children at a very early age. By their teen years, they can teach others, like Umdai taught you."

"I'm from Eregon, here on a mission which has turned into a personal adventure," revealed Wilby. "I have come to return the Rainbow's End to my land."

"Do you so easily confide in a stranger?" asked Kellin.

"No. You are the first one I've ever told about my mission. The King warned me not to say anything. It just slipped out. You won't tell anyone, will you?"

"Your secret is safe with me. So, you're from Eregon. How did you cross the Great River? I've heard that Eregon is still quite a desolate place with no flowers or leaves on the trees, and everything is brown like a dust bowl."

"Yes, to all those things. I have an amulet that helped me get through the wall of water in the middle of the Great River." Wilby pulled the amulet from under her clothes and showed it to Kellin.

Kellin chuckled, her eyes alight with keen awareness. "Don't you see the hand of The Almighty in this?"

"What do you mean?"

Kellin leaned forward to explain. "Look at the timing! I was arrested in the marketplace today and you arrived in time to be my witness. This meeting with me tonight did not happen by coincidence. This is your chance to go through the purple door and climb the Great Mountain. Enter the Rainbow's End and return It to Eregon."

"How do you know these things?" Wilby said in amazement.

"Never mind. We have too little time. The Chancellor is going to the Palace City to consult the Governor. You have the amulet that will open the purple door."

"But this is not the Chancellor's amulet. I received this amulet from Eregon's King. It's not the same."

"Ah, but both amulets came from the same place," remarked Kellin.

"What same place?" asked Wilby. "Where is that?"

They were interrupted by a loud knock on the door. "Time's up!" declared the guard. The door swung open.

Kellin winked at Wilby. "Thank you for visiting me, Wilby," she said. "You remind me so much of my daughter, Umdai. Do say hello to her when you return home. Remember me to your father when you see him. Good-bye."

"My father?" said Wilby. Kellin winked at her again.

"Oh, yes, my father. I'll tell him that you still think well of him. I'll leave the game with you."

"The accused may not have any gifts," stated the guard.

Wilby took apart the twisting maze of Pogran and gathered up all the pieces, wondering at her conversation with Kellin. She hugged Kellin, left the room, and returned to the guard station.

Jahaamaa greeted Wilby, "Well, did you have a good visit? I'm tired. Let's go home now."

"Jahaamaa," Wilby asked, "can we, please, take one more walk by the purple door?"

"Are you crazy? It's nighttime!" Jahaamaa replied. "We saw the purple door this afternoon. Why do you want to see it again?"

"Well," Wilby said, thinking fast, "it is the only place in Neer'stazone with the color purple. So many people come here as pilgrims and never see the color. I could tell people that it does exist when I get back home. Would you do this just for me, please?"

"Oh, all right!" he said. "But we'll have to sneak there. I don't like doing this at night. It's risky. We have to keep both eyes open."

"Well, we have four eyes between the two of us," she said with a giggle. "Let's go."

Jahaamaa and Wilby walked back to the main entrance with the guard. As they were about to leave, Jahaamaa turned to the guard and said, "I think Wilby left her hat back there. Can I go and retrieve it?"

"No, I'll get it," replied the guard.

"Oh, you don't have to bother. I know where she left it. You can trust me; my uncle is the Chancellor!"

"All right, but be back here in ten minutes."

Jahaamaa and Wilby walked down the main hall and then crept through the Court of Uniformity. They entered the Chancellor's chambers and ran down the narrow hallway. Soon, they arrived at the purple door.

"Well, here we are," Jahaamaa said. "Look all you want at the purple door."

Wilby reached beneath her clothing and took out the white amulet. She inserted the amulet into the disc-shaped slot. The door began to hum and shift like liquid amethyst. Then it spread into an open purple arch. On the other side, the set of colored steps appeared just as she had seen that afternoon.

"What did you do?" Jahaamaa gasped at Wilby, for he could hardly believe his eyes. "Where did you get that amulet?"

Wilby passed under the arch. "Come with me, Jahaamaa," she said. "Let's climb the Great Mountain together."

"Wh-what are you saying?" Jahaamaa stammered. "Only the Chancellor may set foot on the Great Mountain. Only he can intercede at the Throne of The Almighty. Did Kellin put these crazy thoughts in your head?"

"No, Jahaamaa," she replied. "I'm from Eregon, and I've come to restore the Rainbow's End to our land. Please come with me."

"Eregon? You're from Eregon? You're going to restore the Rainbow's End to Eregon? I can't believe this! You're a spy?"

ENTERING THE PURPLE DOOR

"I'm not a spy!" retorted Wilby. "After all the time I've spent with you, and you think of me as only a spy? Won't you come with me *now*! Please?"

The sound of other footsteps and voices echoed in the hallway. "I gave them ten minutes, and they didn't come back."

"Let's find out what's going on," another voice said.

"Wilby, I can't come," said Jahaamaa. "I must stay here. Please understand."

"I don't understand, but I must go," Wilby replied.

She reached back and retrieved the white amulet. The purple arch turned back into a door and closed behind her, leaving Jahaamaa alone in the hallway. The disc-shaped slot disappeared, and the purple door was sealed from any further entry.

Jahaamaa scurried toward the other end of the corridor, sneaked back to the entrance, and walked home alone in the dark.

"How much of a twist is this?" he kept muttering to himself. "It's all turned out to be worse."

Chapter Ten

CROSSING PATHS

"Jahaamaa! Come here!" bellowed the Chancellor. "I need to talk to you."

Jahaamaa was halfway through breakfast. He got up from the table and went into the living room. The Chancellor was dressed for traveling.

"What did you do?!!" Chancellor Masiuah thundered at Jahaamaa. "The guards at the Court of Uniformity told me you took a girl to see the purple door last night! That was the second time, wasn't it? After I warned you that visitors aren't allowed there."

"Well, uh, uncle..." said Jahaamaa. "She was a visitor and told me that she could spread the news about how we are favored by The Almighty to see the Great Mountain."

"What did I tell you about that door being off-limits?"

"I'm sorry, uncle, I wasn't thinking."

"You're right, you weren't thinking - the right things. You were thinking about how you might impress your friend. But you didn't think about how to protect our traditions and ways. Didn't you?"

"No, I-I-I guess not," Jahaamaa sputtered.

"Where is that girl now? I must know!" demanded the Chancellor.

"Uh, well, um, she left the city, "replied Jahaamaa.

"All right, never see her again. I forbid it!"

"Uncle, something else. I don't think you should have a trial with this Kellin."

"What!!" exclaimed the Chancellor. "We have our laws, boy, and this woman has broken them. This is a very serious crime. Did that girl charm you into thinking this?"

"Uh, no, I mean, Kellin has a good point about things being different."

"That's all wishful thinking, Jahaamaa. I raised you ever since you were a little boy and taught you all that you need to know. Are you questioning me or our laws?"

"Well, I think that maybe this time, it's a little, a little...." Jahaamaa stammered.

"A little what? Too much? I'll tell you what to think, don't question it."

"Uncle, I'm going to leave now," Jahaama replied. "I need to have some time with my own thoughts."

"Where are you going?"

"I think I'll go visit my best friend, Wozner. He invited me to stay over for a few days."

The Chancellor stared at Jahaamaa and scowled. "Okay, go visit your friend Wozner. Clear your head. Get all of this nonsense out of your mind before you come back."

"I'll pack now. Goodbye, Uncle."

"I'll see you when you get back. Now, I'll get ready for my own trip," replied the Chancellor.

"Your highness. Excuse me, your highness," said Nupa, the Governor's attendant.

The Governor was slumped on his throne, napping. "Yes, what is it?" He rubbed the sleep from his eyes.

"There's an applicant for the Royal Gardener position here to see you."

"Another one? Haven't we seen enough?"

"This one is different, sire. This one insisted on seeing you. He used your middle name."

"He used my *middle* name? Are you sure?"

"Yes, sire."

"Well, show him in!"

Nupa hurried away and returned with Bilnot following him.

"Sire, this is Bilnot. He is a gardener from Amudia, Chancellor Masuiah's district. He wants to apply for the Royal Gardener position."

"Bilnot. Bilnot? That name seems familiar. From Chancellor Masuiah's district? Oh, I remember; you're the Bilnot who won the Uniformity Award from Masuiah, aren't you?"

Bilnot bowed low and removed his brown leather hat. "Yes, your honor, I am. I come from a long line of gardeners, from my great-great-great grandfathers. I would like to serve you and Neer'stazone as the Royal Gardener."

"Humph," uttered the Governor. "Perhaps we can talk more privately. Nupa, leave us alone for a time."

Nupa bowed low and left the throne room.

When they were alone, the Governor spoke softly. "Well, Bilnot, here we are. I wondered when our paths would cross again,"

"It has been some time, hasn't it?" replied Bilnot.

"You do remember our days together in Eregon, don't you? We were going to change things there, and to our surprise, the twists in fate were more than we could imagine."

The Governor rose and walked toward Bilnot. "You know that we both followed the Rainbow's End here to Neer'stazone, but you were not able to grasp it, were you?"

"Neither were you. So now we're here and not in Eregon."

"Neither of us has done badly; in fact, I became Governor and you still are a gardener. An excellent gardener, if not the best, like you were in Eregon," said the Governor. "Don't you miss your family?"

"I don't remember my family. I've been in a daze, like a dream, since we left the Kingdom. It's as if I have just awakened."

"When we pursued the Rainbow's End, we gave up our way of life for the higher mission. Look at what we've gained here. We could never have had these riches, power, or glory in Eregon. And now look: Eregon's a wasteland."

"We couldn't return there, could we?" asked Bilnot. "It's too late and the time of separation has been too great. I regret not coming to know my family. And for me, I've perfected my gardening skills. I guess that's why I'm here."

"Yes, Bilnot. Your timing is perfect, like always. The Royal Gardens are in shambles. The last four gardeners from the Guild have not taken uniformity seriously. I'm convinced that the Royal

Gardens should be an example to the entire Kingdom. Citizens will visit them and marvel at the perfection that we can attain. Even Chancellor Masuiah may shift the standard of the Code of Uniformity from Amudia to the Palace City. Then, everyone in the land will understand by having our flowers alike we are one people. Our uniformity will have great power—the power over people's imaginations and their spirits."

"If I may help you in that quest, the people would hail you as a genius," Bilnot replied. "I can start soon, depending on your wish."

The Governor reflected for a moment and then raised his head. He looked Bilnot in the eyes and said, "Start immediately. You have even my army to help you in rebuilding the Royal Gardens."

"I must go into the country for a few days," Bilnot replied. "I want to see my meadows again, one last time, before I begin work on the Royal Gardens."

"You have my permission to go. When will you return?"

"Give me two weeks, and I will return."

"Go then. I will wait for your return to transform our land."

Bilnot left and went to his home in Amudia. He put away his shears from his holster and inserted his digging trowel instead. He retrieved his backpack from under his bed and dumped its contents on the floor. He sorted through the seeds and bulbs.

"This is the one," he said, holding up a large, oval-shaped bulb. He slipped it into his pocket and put all of the others back into the pack, which he slung over his shoulder.

Bilnot gathered provisions for a two-week journey; then, he set out on foot for the country. As he passed through the red gate of Amudia, a grand caravan exited, too. A coach decorated with flower streamers, each consisting of precisely 125 five-petal flowers, plodded through the gate.

It's Masuiah! thought Bilnot. He skirted behind the crowd and slipped away unnoticed.

Masuiah's entourage continued to the Palace City. Masuiah strode furiously into the Majestic Hall, where he summoned the Captain of the Guard.

"I must see the Governor **immediately**!" the Chancellor shouted. "I-M-M-E-D-I-A-T-E-L-Y!!"

The Captain disappeared toward the Throne Room, leaving the Chancellor pacing in the Majestic Hall.

Shortly, the Captain reappeared and said, "The Governor can see you now."

"It's about time," Masuiah rasped. He strode past the Captain, who sprinted to keep up with him. The Captain paused to knock when they arrived at the Throne Room, but Masuiah thrust the door open and entered. The Governor, perched on the Throne, stared at him.

"What is the meaning of this interruption?" When Masuiah didn't answer, the Governor glowered and dismissed the Captain of the Royal Guard. "Now, what is the trouble, Chancellor?"

"What's the trouble? What's the trouble! Why, much is the trouble! Don't you know what's going on in your own Kingdom?"

"What is going on in my own Kingdom, Masuiah?" grunted the Governor.

"See what I mean? There's an uprising in the land. A woman gardener, Kellin, is subverting the Kingdom! She has flagrantly violated the Code of Uniformity through her 'Hope Patch.' Now the whole Gardener's Guild is in an uproar, and we're going to lose control of everything we worked so hard for."

"What is a 'Hope Patch?'"

"I have evidence that this Hope Patch is a hidden garden that defies us and mocks our way of life. It is a breeding ground that threatens the very foundation of our order. Our society, based on the five royal colors, is in jeopardy."

"How do you know this?"

"We found a note in her own handwriting where she calls this garden her 'secret plot.' It's a plot all right—a plot against us! She's hoping to twist the order and turn against the land. This is treason, I tell you."

"Treason is a serious charge!" replied the Governor. "Are you sure?"

"She is subverting the order of our Kingdom and our way of life," Masuiah continued. "Imagine what would happen if other women did what she did! Imagine if our young people, especially the teens, learned that the five royal colors were no longer our standard way of life. Imagine if our very symbol of our Kingdom as a paradise, a garden, were completely out of control!"

"We would have chaos!" said the Governor, frowning. "Everything would change—our education, our meadows and markets, even the way we design and build our cities! Tell me, Chancellor, you found no purple flowers there, did you?"

"Well, no! I did not personally visit this plot and I hope not for all of our sakes. It's bad enough to have treason; we don't need apostasy. You've read the Scrolls of Eregon. You know that purple is the color closest to The Almighty's Throne. If we grew purple flowers in the land, why, we'd insult the Sovereign One. That was the downfall of Eregon, you know."

"We can't let that happen here," replied the Governor. "After all, there is only one Rainbow's End left."

"We must stop this plot immediately!" said Masuiah. "We must snuff out any semblance of a movement. We must have order and control, or we will perish. I've arrested this Kellin and am holding her in Amudia."

"Aren't you the Chancellor? Isn't the Court of Uniformity in Amudia, as well? You have my authority to try this Kellin and punish her for these crimes."

"Very well," replied Masuiah. "The Court will try her for sabotage, treason, and subverting our Kingdom. I want to make a public example of her behavior, so that no one will ever again attempt what she has done."

"You have my permission to do whatever you want; however, do not harm her physically. You would have an even worse riot if all the women in the Kingdom saw that she was being harmed."

"I have the perfect punishment in mind," said Masuiah. "I will return to Amudia immediately and begin preparations. I would like you to be there when I announce her sentence."

"I will attend Kellin's trial and defend the Code of Uniformity," said the Governor. "We must have order; *we* must have control."

"Excellent! I will send you a messenger when everything is ready. Farewell."

Masuiah strutted from the Throne Room into the Main Hall. He exited the Palace, entered his carriage, and returned to Amudia with his entourage.

Within three days, Bilnot arrived at his meadow, the prize-winning garden of Neer'stazone. This meadow had won ten consecutive district Uniformity awards. Now Bilnot was about to do something that would not win any awards, at least not from the Court of Uniformity.

Purple must now replace red.

The phrase from last night's vivid dream echoed in Bilnot's head. He had slept restlessly. In the middle of the night, he dreamed that he was standing before a large crowd of people, too large to count. Each person held a different flower of different colors and shapes.

Kellin was there, too. She was directing the people to change places, depending on the color of their flowers. It was like watching a flag wave as the people moved from one place to another. Those standing in the back switched places with those standing in front: exchanging purple with red, blue with orange, green with yellow. All stayed and no one left.

Bilnot woke up in a sweat, disturbed by the sudden reversals in direction.

Purple must now replace red!

The thought became a mantra, repeating with each step he took. He walked through the meadow to its center, a shallow depression, where the red five-petal pansies grew in a thick ring.

Purple must now replace red. The thought shouted in Bilnot's head. *Purple must now replace red!*

He removed his trowel and neatly dug up several red pansy plants. Taking the one large, oval bulb from his pocket, he planted it in place of the pansies. He smoothed out the ground with dirt and walked toward the edge of his meadow. As he reached the road, a shoot broke through the soil where he had planted the large oval bulb.

"I don't understand why he is always so mean," Jahaamaa told Lady Trentum. "I tried to follow every word my uncle said until I met Wilby."

"Jahamma," she replied. "I don't understand that man either. It's like he has fallen so much in love with his own way of thinking that he can't accept a different point of view."

"Exactly! When I told him that I thought that Kellin didn't do anything wrong, he got very angry. At first, I thought that Kellin was bringing trouble to our land, but now I think she is right. He was so angry that I showed Wilby the purple door a second time. She actually opened that door and went through it. She asked me to come, but I didn't. Now I wish I had gone with her."

"Hmmm. I think you like Wilby, Jahaamaa."

"Well, I do like her, but I don't understand her either. I don't seem to fit in anywhere. Maybe I should just go away and be alone."

Lady Trentum stroked Jahaamas's hair. "I think you are a fine, brave young man. I would be happy to call you my son, just like Wil, Wes, and Wozner. Wozner really likes you. He's soft-hearted – learn from him. You carry more love inside your heart than you realize right now. One day, you'll lead others with your love. You are welcome to be part of our family and stay as long as you want."

"Thank you," Jahaamaa choked back his tears. "I'd like to stay with you for a while."

Chapter Eleven

TRIALS ON THE JOURNEY

It was early morning when Wilby arrived at the base of the Great Mountain. She had climbed the rough, colored stone steps and passed where Masuiah would stop to pray.

The mountain's high top was cloaked with clouds. Wilby surveyed the rocky terrain, looking for a route. Three desert pine trees rustled in the breeze about one hundred yards ahead. Wilby began to scramble over the rocks toward the trees. The ascent was gradual, and Wilby reached the trees shortly.

A path began at the base of the middle tree and led farther up the Great Mountain. Wilby followed the trail. The climb became steeper. The rocky ground gave way to boulders and crags; Wilby's pace slowed considerably. Her muscles ached, and she was drenched with sweat.

This is so much harder than I ever dreamed it would be, she worried.

She began to doubt if she should have taken this mission at all. She felt the pain of Jahaamaa's charges of being a spy. *Was Kellin really right? Where was Wozner; what was he doing? Wouldn't it have been better to stay home with Gramma?*

The breeze changed direction and blew at Wilby's back, cooling the perspiration that soaked her clothing. She kept going as her stomach churned with anxiety. By mid-morning, Wilby reached a broad plateau.

She paused to rest, looking back over the forest at the base of the Great Mountain. The breeze had become still. The boulders at the edges of the plateau dwarfed her.

The mission is nearly over. Wilby thought about the events that had led to the present moment: the meeting with the King; the encounters with Wozner and the Great Viceroy; the episode with the gardener; the Governor's feast.

She thought again about Jahaamaa and then about Kellin's strange remark about her father, whom she did not remember. Most of all, she thought about the puzzling changes of the amulet.

I'm on the last leg of the journey, about to find the Rainbow's End. Encouraged by the hope that she would soon complete her mission, Wilby walked across the plateau. The rocks above thrust upward like sheer walls; there was no place to climb.

Wilby searched the north end of the plateau to no avail. There, too, the rocks were smooth and vertical. After an hour of surveying the way up, Wilby leaned against the rocky wall. She felt like she had failed. There was no place to go but down.

Clink. Clink, clink. A small stone bounced down the rocky wall and landed on the plateau about ten feet from Wilby. *Clunk. Clunk, clunk.* Wilby looked up and saw a massive boulder bouncing directly at her.

Suddenly, a blast of wind knocked Wilby over, pushing her out of the way. The boulder landed with a crash and shook the ground where she had been standing.

Whew! Was that close!

Bruised from her fall, Wilby looked up at the spot above the boulder. About ten feet from the plateau, there was a crevice that seemed to widen as it went up the face of the wall.

Wilby scrambled on top of the boulder and reached the crevice. She found a handhold and grunted as she strained to pull herself up. Then, she stretched upward to another crack. The crevice widened as she climbed, and the holds became more frequent. After seventy feet, the crevice turned into a stony path that led farther up the mountain.

When she reached the stony path, Wilby found a large rock and sat down. *This climb is tiring. I need to rest for a while.*

A gentle breeze streamed over her body as she stretched out under the sunlight. *This feels good.* She dozed off and dreamed about Hdora. Rhima and Andrew were about to have their daily dance about how much bread is left at the end of the day. But this time, the bakery shelves were loaded with loaves. The flowerbed in the village square was full of colorful flowers. The green leaves on the bushes were vibrant and full. Gramma was there, tending the flowers. *Gramma, how much I miss Gramma!*

Wilby woke suddenly. "I better keep going now, so I can reach the Rainbow's End and get home to Gramma," she mumbled.

TRIALS ON THE JOURNEY

The day of Kellin's trial arrived. She was taken by cart to the City Hall at dawn and reached the temple that housed the Court of Uniformity. The Captain of the Uniformity Police led Kellin into the Court and stationed her at the defendant's stand. The Governor had come from the Palace City to witness the trial, just like he promised.

The judgment bench sat in the middle of the Court of Uniformity. The bench was shaped like a half-circle made of five panels. There was one panel colored blue, another green, and others of yellow, orange, and red. Masuiah sat on the judgment bench whenever the Court was in session, wearing the Court Glove of Judgment over his white-gloved right hand.

The Court Glove of Judgment was specially designed, with each finger dyed in one of the five royal colors. The thumb was red; the forefinger was orange; the middle finger was yellow; the ring finger was green, and the little finger was blue.

Masuiah wore the glove to make solemn pronouncements and to deliver sentences. His fist would strike the top of the bench to get everyone's attention when he was ready to speak. He hummed the little rhyme to himself as he sat down:

"Five fingers and five toes:

Five petals that flowers grow.

Five colors and that's it -

keeps us all so close-knit."

The Court of Uniformity convened with the trial of Kellin in the main courtroom. Unlike previous trials, Masuiah did not seek the wisdom of The Almighty at the foot of the Great Mountain before this trial. This time, he knew the outcome he wanted.

The Code of Uniformity

1. All flowers have only 5 petals.
2. The color purple is not allowed in the land.
3. Gardens must be uniform in size and shape.
4. Only the Royal Guild grows flowers.
5. Flowers can only be grown in approved meadows.
6. Violators of the Code of Uniformity will be punished.
7. The Governor and Chancellor will judge all violations in the Court of Uniformity.

THE CODE OF UNIFORMITY

The large doors were open to the courtyard, filled with citizens from all over Neer'stazone. The Governor's prosecutor read the list of charges:

- conspiracy to undermine the Code of Uniformity;
- treason;
- subverting the Land of Neer'stazone with varieties of flowers that were not on the approved list of the Gardener's Guild,
- and violating the Kingdom's five Royal colors.

These were very grave accusations. All the while, Kellin remained silent, her eyes fixed on the floor.

The advocate assigned to Kellin arose and approached the Chancellor. He drew a deep breath and began his defense.

"Your honors, great Chancellor, gentlemen and women of the Court, indeed, of the Kingdom. We are gathered to hear the case of the Kingdom of Neer'stazone against Kellin, a Royal Gardener of great loyalty and service to our land. She has served many, many years in making our land one of beauty and delight."

"The charges of treason, subversion, and violations of the Code of Uniformity are indeed serious," the advocate continued. "However, where is the proof of these charges? Who can know the heart of a person—a person's inner thoughts or beliefs? Who has seen these violations of flora and color? Where are Neer'stazone's witnesses to these things? I submit that Kellin is innocent—there is no proof of these accusations."

The prosecutor interrupted, "Do you want proof? Dozens of people heard her speak against the Code of Uniformity when she overturned flower carts in our marketplace. But even more, we have undeniable proof that Kellin is a threat to our very way of life, our dearly held law. I call the Kingdom's first witness. I call Rucda of the Royal Guild of Gardeners."

A burly man stood and approached the judgment bench.

"Put both hands on the image of the Rainbow's End and say after me, 'I swear to say the utmost truth by the breath of The Almighty,'" said Masuiah.

"I so swear," replied Rucda. He walked to the witness stand.

"Rucda, on the evening of Tuesday, three weeks ago, were you present at a meeting of the Royal Guild of Gardeners in the Earthworks Tavern?"

"Yes, I was."

"And do you remember who else was there?"

"Well, the entire Guild of Gardeners was meeting there."

"What was the purpose of that meeting?"

"The President of the Guild told us of the Governor's displeasure with the performance of the Royal Gardens. We were told that the Governor was looking for greater conformance in the Royal Gardens and that he was unhappy with the past four gardeners who worked there."

"I see. And what was the result?"

"I don't really know. Most of the Guild broke up into small groups and talked among themselves about the situation."

"Rucda, did you see the accused, Kellin, there?"

"Yes, she was there. She talked to several members of the Guild and spent considerable time speaking with Bilnot."

"Did you hear any of her conversation with Bilnot?"

"Yes, I did. They talked about the Royal Gardens and the open position of the chief gardener for the Governor."

"Was there anything else?"

"Why, yes. Kellin told Bilnot about a secret plot; she called it a Hope Patch where she was growing all sorts of flowers of every shape and color."

"She called it a secret plot, did she?"

"Yes, that's what she called it—a secret plot."

The chief prosecutor turned to the Chancellor and said, "I have no more questions."

"The witness may step down," Masuiah commanded.

"Doesn't my defendant Kellin get a chance to cross-examine the witness?" asked defense counsel.

"No, she has no chance," replied Masuiah. "This is not an ordinary trial with give-and-take protocol. This is a tribunal, investigating high crimes against the state. Call the next witness."

"I call Bilnot to the stand," cried the prosecutor. "Bilnot, come forward."

Silence filled the courtroom; no one stirred.

"I call Bilnot to the stand!" repeated the prosecutor. "Where is Bilnot?"

There was no answer in the courtroom, and no one came forward. All of the people began looking around and whispering that Bilnot was absent.

"Where is Bilnot?!!" shouted the prosecutor.

"It appears that Bilnot is not here," observed Masuiah with a snarl. "Perhaps he is on a journey or sleeping. Call louder, maybe you can awaken him."

"BILNOT!!!"

"Stop it!" shouted Masuiah. "Order in the Court! Order, I say. We'll proceed without Bilnot's testimony. Haven't you additional evidence, a note to Bilnot with Kellin's own handwriting on it?"

"Yes, your Honor," replied the prosecutor. "I have a note that we found in Bilnot's lodge here in the Gate City."

"Bring it forward," said Masuiah.

Kellin held her breath as the prosecutor retrieved a folded note, covered with dust, and placed it on the judgment bench in front of Masuiah.

"Let's read what this note says, shall we?" Masuiah smiled as he read:

Dear Bilnot,

I'm sorry that I can't be with you this morning. An emergency came up. I've drawn a map to my secret plot. Still think that there are only five royal colors? Wait until you see this garden. I call it my "Hope Patch." Get there before the sun has fully risen. Stay there as long as you like, but destroy the map before leaving. I'll talk with you soon to learn about your experience. Kellin

"Do you have the map to this Hope Patch?" asked the Chancellor.

"Your Honor, we did not find such a map anywhere in Bilnot's house," replied the prosecutor. "However, Kellin did write about a secret plot, a Hope Patch. We now have definite evidence that she is conspiring against the Governor."

"Your Honor," interrupted the defense counsel. "Shall we hear what *Kellin* has to say? Even in the Code of Uniformity, the arrested have a right to speak at a tribunal. Shall all the people of Neer'stazone be silenced when they have a day in Court?"

"All right!" conceded Masuiah. "I call Kellin to state her defense."

Kellin walked to the front of the courtroom and stared at Masuiah.

"I will defend myself," Kellin replied. "May I speak freely, so that the breath of The Almighty may guide my words and utter the truth. Your honors, people of the Court, and all citizens of Neer'stazone: I have tended flowers of many shapes and sizes, colors and hues since my childhood. Those flowers have grown here for ages. It has only been in recent times that the Code of Uniformity was written and imposed upon this land. You all know that the meadows were full of many blossoms that grew exceedingly well here. It was only through fear that the meadows would be trampled and picked clean, that the Code was created. It was not that way in the beginning."

"As a gardener, I have prepared the soil, nurtured seeds, planted, watered, pruned and gazed upon such great beauty," she continued. "The flowers don't need the Code of Uniformity; they are perfect and beautiful as they are, each in its own way. Each blossom, each petal, is created by The Almighty. There are never too few or too many petals. And there are far more than the five royal colors—"

"Blasphemy! Blasphemy!" shouted the Governor, jumping from his seat. "You all heard her. We have our Code and with It, we honor the Throne of The Almighty."

"Twists and turns!" cried Kellin. "You've twisted my words and turned them against me. Let me finish. I am not finished!"

"Oh yes, you are!" exclaimed the Chancellor. "You are finished! We will have no more of this! This trial is over! I find you guilty as charged. Bring her to me."

The court guard seized Kellin and dragged her to the judgment bench. He pushed her to her knees. The Chancellor stood and raised his right hand, garbed with the Court Glove of Judgment. He lowered that hand over Kellin and pronounced the sentence:

"What is alike is one. How good it is. What is one is good and pleasing to The Almighty."

"This is the truth found in our sacred Scroll. The Code of Uniformity dates back to ancient times. This Code is supreme, as Supreme and Everlasting as the Throne of The Almighty. We must obey its truth and please The Almighty with our obedience. Those who don't obey will bring trouble to the land."

The Chancellor paused to be sure everyone was listening. He intended to make an example of Kellin so no one else would dare challenge the Code.

"I find you guilty of treason, subverting the land, and betraying the Code of Uniformity," Masuiah said. "I hereby sentence you to spend the rest of your waking days weaving flower petals into garlands in a cage on public display. You shall travel from town to town and village to village, throughout the land. All the people of Neer'stazone will see how foolish it is to oppose our Code. I have spoken. Take her away."

The court guard led Kellin away. A short time later, he took her to the market of Amudia, where the Chancellor was waiting. The guard pushed her in front of a giant cage constructed of iron bars and mounted on an ordinary flower cart. Like the purple door, the cell door had a slot; Masuiah unlocked the cage with his amulet.

"Put her in and get her working!" he ordered. The guards put Kellin inside, and Masuiah locked the door.

"There is no way out for you now, Kellin," said the Chancellor. "Only this amulet will unlock the door."

Then he went away to his chambers. The guards began heaping flower blossoms between the bars into the cage. The citizens of Amudia taunted her until sunset, laughing at the thousands of petals she must now weave into floral garlands.

Chapter Twelve

Reaching the Summit

By nightfall, Wilby had made immense progress. Her face, arms, and legs were coated with dirt from the mountain trail. The sky had cleared, and the stars shone brightly in the distance.

Directly overhead, the clouds still circled the mountain's top. The bright colors of the Rainbow's End shone from around the edges of the mountainside. Wilby found a place to rest and fell into a deep sleep. She dreamed that she was in a garden full of different colored and shaped flowers. The gardener Kellen from Vdious was there, lecturing on the beauty of diversity. Behind the gardener, there was a waterfall that looked like the Rainbow's End.

Different stripes of colors were flowing in the waterfall. The water gurgled and looked refreshing. But when she approached the waterfall, three stones blocked the way. She started around them, but they changed positions and formed a barrier when she tried to move closer. The dream repeated itself throughout the night.

Wilby woke at the morning's light with the dream still vivid in her mind. She stretched her arms and legs; she was hungry and thirsty. Wilby rummaged in her pack and pulled out the last bit of bread Jahaamaa had given. She munched, savoring her last morsel.

She squeezed the dew from the leaves of a nearby bush into her hand and lapped up the water. Then, she began to climb the stone path. After about an hour, she came to a junction. One side led west; the other east. Both trails disappeared around the mountainside, and both paths looked inviting. Wilby was stumped.

Which way?

After a short time, something like a small light seemed to flicker farther up among the rocks of the eastern path. Wilby clambered to the spot. It was a small bush whose silver leaves curled in the breeze. The trail appeared to move across the mountain to a ridge.

Wilby continued the climb and reached the ridge. She crept along the ridge as it became narrower and narrower. Finally, the ridge broadened to a small flat area about three feet square. At the edge was a sheer drop-off. Ten feet away, the path continued. A vertical chimney of rock was above her. There was no other way to go.

Jump! JUMP! Wilby's thoughts screamed at her. But out loud, she said, "Are you crazy? There's no way to jump across this chasm."

JUMP! J - U - M - P!

More insistent it became. Wilby remembered the Seer's words: listen to what's inside you. "But should I jump or not? Ten feet is too far; I might make six feet. This really could be the end of the journey."

REACHING THE SUMMIT

Wilby stretched her legs and tried to clear her mind. "If I'm meant to reach the Rainbow's End, there will be a way to do this," she said.

She searched again but found no other way. *Jump, Wilby.* That sounded like Jahaamaa's voice. *Just jump.*

Wilby shivered with fear. Then, she remembered how she would skip between rocks in Hdora. As a child, she would place the stones farther apart to jump. When she would land on them, Wilby stretched her jumping ability. She drew back against the mountain wall, relaxing her muscles. She crouched into a jumping position.

Wilby took a step and leaped toward the path with a loud yell. A blast of wind rocketed down the chimney rock and ricocheted from the platform. It caught Wilby mid-air and propelled her over the chasm. Wilby landed six feet from the edge in the middle of the path.

After she regained her breath, Wilby scrambled up the path toward the mountaintop. As she got closer, the clouds surrounding the peak engulfed her. She could only see enough of the way to take one step, one step. One step. One step. One step. She continued at this slow, unknowing pace.

After a long while, she reached the top of the Great Mountain. The wind began to blow, swirling the clouds around Wilby. The clouds became lighter, and patches of blue sky appeared. Soon, the clouds had retreated toward the sky, and Wilby could see all the surrounding countryside.

There were farms and roads. The Great River and the forests of Neer'stazone. Even more giant mountains loomed far off toward the north. There were towns, too. The palaces of Eregon and Neer'stazone were like tiny dots on the landscape.

There are no divisions in the land. The only walls were built by people. "Everything is part of one land," she exclaimed.

Shphmn. Shphmn. The amulet on Wilby's chest began to vibrate. Slowly, the fifth arc was swept with a blue color. Now the colors on the amulet were red, orange, yellow, green, and blue.

It's like the land, Wilby thought. *Green earth, blue sky—united.* Wilby looked down toward the west. Below her on a plateau was the Rainbow's End, shining in the sun.

A waterfall fell from the plateau, forming a stream at the base of the Great Mountain. The stream fed into the Great River in the distance. A path shaped like a rocky stairway led directly to the plateau.

"What am I waiting for?" she said aloud as she headed down the staircase, one step at a time.

The Uniformity Awards Committee left Amudia and traveled to Bilnot's prize meadow. With Kellin's conviction, Masuiah wanted to re-establish the great value of uniformity in the land's meadows. Bilnot had received ten consecutive district Uniformity Awards, and now was the time to bestow a special honor, Favor of the Kingdom, upon him.

By publicly recognizing how Bilnot's meadow proved that everything was alike, Masuiah would remove any doubts about what was allowed to grow in Neer'stazone.

There were five people on the committee. Each one was learned in one of the five pure colors of the Code of Uniformity. A large delegation of loyal citizens accompanied them. After traveling for four hours, they arrived at Bilnot's meadow.

They were impressed by the immaculate condition of the field, its waves of five-petal flowers, all of the purest hues of red, yellow, orange, green, and blue. The flowers were arranged in concentric rings with blue flowers at the outermost edge. A path cut through the meadow to its center.

"Ah! Now we see the perfection that creation was meant to have!" exclaimed one of the committee members.

"Yes," replied another. "Soil clear of debris. Five-petal flowers so neatly arranged and flawlessly spaced."

"Glory to Masuiah!" shouted a third. "We are viewing a master's hand of gardening."

The blue specialist measured and compared the blue hue to the Code Standard. So did the green, yellow, and orange specialists. All of the flowers matched the Code exactly. The committee was ecstatic, and the large crowd clapped loudly at each color match. They walked to the center of the meadow, where the thick ring of five-petal red pansies bloomed. The red specialist bent down to examine the red flowers but halted abruptly. Amid the red pansies stood a three-foot-tall dark-purple tulip waving defiantly in the breeze. All six petals were fully open, like an open hand stretching out in all directions - to the sky, the land, and all around.

"What in The Almighty's Name is that?" cried the red specialist.

"Purple? This is purple!" exclaimed the blue specialist. "A purple flower!"

"But purple is outlawed!" blurted out one of the three pilgrims who had come to Amudia. "What is a purple flower, with six petals, doing in Bilnot's meadow?"

"It must be a conspiracy," said the green committee member. "This must be the work of Kellin, who was just convicted of treason."

They stood in stunned silence, unable to move. A stir ran through the crowd, creating rumors about a purple, six-petal flower amid a thick ring of five-petal red pansies.

"What could this mean?" asked a leading woman from the nearest town. "Isn't purple the color of The Almighty? Is it a sign? Is The Almighty present among us?"

Another added, "If it is from The Almighty, let me touch it!"

The crowd pressed closer to the pansies, and the committee formed a ring around the purple flower.

"Don't touch it!" cried the Chairperson of the committee. "Anyone who touches this flower may anger The Almighty!"

The crowd fell back, unsure of what to do. People began to sit down in the meadow, waiting for something to happen. Meanwhile, the news spread throughout the neighboring towns and villages about a six-petal dark-purple flower growing in the middle of Bilnot's prized meadow.

One committee member, accompanied by several townspeople, hurried back to Amudia to inform Masuiah of the news.

Chapter Thirteen

A Kiss for the Tulips

Masuiah became livid with anger when he heard the story and how the people were speculating on the purple flower's meaning. "It's nothing!" he bellowed. "A quirk, a peculiarity! I will put a stop to this foolishness myself!"

And so, Masuiah gathered the best people in his Uniformity Police and traveled to Bilnot's meadow. The roads were jammed full of people from all over Neer'stazone. All of the blossoms in Bilnot's meadow became trampled by pilgrims who had come to see the six-petal, dark-purple flower. Masuiah and the Uniformity Police forced their way to the middle of the meadow where the Awards Committee still guarded the dark-purple tulip. Jahaamaa and Wozner, who had heard the rumors, worked their way to the front row of the crowd.

Masuiah looked around him at those who had gathered. He bent over and looked at the dark-purple tulip carefully. Then he motioned the Uniformity Police to clear all people from the rear portion of the meadow.

He addressed the crowd in a loud voice: "Citizens of Neer'stazone, friends from far and wide!" he cried. "Why have you come here? Have you come to see a flower? A tall, proud flower with six petals and a dark purple color? I have heard it said that many of you think this flower has special powers, that it is a sign of The Almighty's presence!"

"Why do you think and believe these thoughts? The Throne of The Almighty is in the heavens, not in the dirt of the land! Do you forget our Code of Uniformity? Do you forget our traditions? Do you forget how our meadows, gardens, and forests reflect only the pure colors of the Rainbow's End? Do you forget that we dishonor The Almighty when we seek superstition instead of order; when we seek signs instead of valuing our heritage?"

"Citizens of Neer'stazone, I ask you to think of where we are. We are in the middle of the meadow of the great gardener, Bilnot, who is about to receive the Favor of the Kingdom award, the highest award one can earn. His meadow is the premier example of uniformity. Look around you now. Notice each five-petal flower, its shape, and color. Perfect, aren't they?"

"What about the purple flower?" one of the pilgrims asked. "Isn't purple the sign of The Almighty's Presence?"

Masuiah looked around angrily, "Don't you remember the story that I taught you of what happened to Eregon? Don't you heed its lesson? That place had purple flowers growing all over it. Tulips, irises, lilac bushes, lilies, and morning glories. And now what does it look like? It's a dust bowl; there are no flowers there at all. They insulted the Throne of The Almighty by making purple as common as the grass. Is that what you want to happen here in Neer'stazone?"

"I will show you what I will do with what you think is The Almighty's presence!" he continued in a measured voice.

With a quick move, his left hand ripped the stem of the dark-purple tulip from the earth. He held the tulip high for everyone to see.

"Is the Throne of The Almighty present in a purple flower—present here in the land?" Silence greeted his question.

He chuckled. "Let's see, shall we?"

Using his right hand, still wearing its white glove, he tore the first petal from the tulip and roared, "The Almighty is present!"

The air was utterly still; nothing happened.

He pulled the second petal from the tulip and echoed, "The Almighty is not!"

The crowd stirred restlessly.

Masuiah pulled the third and fourth petals from the tulip, repeating the exact words.

Finally, he pulled the fifth petal and shouted, "The Almighty is *present?*"

The last purple petal limply clasped its stem. With a loud laugh, he plucked the last petal and announced triumphantly, "The Almighty is NOT!"

He looked around at the crowd, who silently bowed their heads in shame. Tears filled the eyes of those who had come expecting a miracle.

"You see, The Almighty is not here," Masuiah said. "Go home. Forget about this purple nonsense. *What is alike is one. How good it is. What is one is good, and pleasing to The Almighty.* The Code of Uniformity is our law and our legend. We rule ourselves. Now go home."

Masuiah took the handful of dark-purple tulip petals and tossed them toward the sky. "Let the wind blow these to The Almighty's Throne!" he shouted.

Just as he said this, a blast of wind rifled through the crowd and caught the purple petals mid-air, tumbling them toward the rear of the meadow.

The people began to disperse. But as the petals came to rest on the trampled dirt of the field, something extraordinary happened. The petals lodged in the soil, immediately sprouting roots and shoots! The shoots multiplied into blossoming six-petal, dark-purple tulips. There were now six of these tulips scattered in the rear of Bilnot's meadow.

"Look!" gasped Wozner to Jahaamaa, when he saw what happened. "It *is* a miracle, Jahaamaa—more dark-purple flowers!"

Wozner sprinted to the first purple tulip and bent down to the ground. "This flower is so beautiful! I've never seen purple or six petals before!" he exclaimed.

"I love you," he whispered as he kissed the tulip.

Make a wish. Go ahead and ask for something good to happen, his soft heart spoke to him. Wozner closed his eyes and thought for a moment. "I have two wishes. I wish that everyone was happy and I wish that Wilby would find a home."

Then he blew gently on the dark-purple petals. The petals began to tingle and shimmer as if they could feel the love in Wozner's heart. Then, the petals let go of the tulip stem and floated up in the breeze, twirling and turning somersaults, dancing in the breeze.

The petals skimmed the soil and planted themselves in the dirt. Suddenly, roots and shoots formed, and six more new, dark-purple six-petal tulips burst forth. For indeed, the glory of The Almighty was present in the dirt of the land. It had now become holy ground.

"The Almighty *IS* present!" he cried. "Jahaamaa! Wil! Wes! Come help me!"

The teens ran to the spot.

"What do we do?" asked Jahaamaa.

"Kiss the tulips, make a wish, ask for something good to happen, and then blow on them," smiled Wozner.

"Are you crazy? Flowers don't have feelings," retorted Jahaamaa.

"These ones do. Just trust yourself and the Breath of The Almighty."

"It's so odd, so different from what I was raised to believe." *You carry more love inside your heart than you realize right now. One day, you'll lead others with your love.* The words of Wozner's mom came back to him. Jahaamaa choked away his tears.

"Yes, I'll do it!"

Jahaamaa knelt over one of the dark-purple tulips, kissed it, and whispered, "I love you. I wish my uncle would be more kind." His teardrop landed softly in the heart of the tulip. Then, he blew gently on the purple petals.

Wil and Wes got down on their knees and did the same. The tulip stems released the dark-purple petals. Like before, they danced in the breeze, and landed, bursting and blooming into new dark-purple tulips.

"Wait until Mom and Dad hear about what you did, Wozner," Wes teased. "You wore your heart on your sleeve again. They will be so proud of you."

"We are too!" added Wes.

"Let's do more," said Jahaamaa.

So, the teens kept kissing the tulips, making wishes, asking for something good to happen, and blowing on the petals. The dark-purple tulips continued to spread throughout the meadow.

The crowd turned and stared at the boys.

"Do you believe that?" gasped the onlookers. "The boys are kissing the tulips and making them spread."

Masuiah, who had reached the road, heard the outcry and stopped. He and the Uniformity Police ran back toward the site. "Grab them!" Masuiah commanded.

Another pilgrim, Jiana, the short, round woman, seized Wozner, but it was too late. Humik and the friends that Wilby and Jahaamaa met on their journey arrived.

"Hey, it's Jahaamaa!" cried Humik. "Jahaamaa, we are your friends and we are here to help you. What should we do?"

"Quick!" said Jahaamaa. "Find a tulip. Kiss it. Make a wish. Ask for something good to happen. Then, blow on the petals."

His friends ran to the other tulips and did the same thing.

"Scriggle Forever!" they shouted.

Carol and Jacqui saw them from their spot in the crowd.

"That's Jahaamaa, the Chancellor's nephew!" Jacqui said. "He *is* good-looking."

"And he's a leader too," added Carol. "I'm sick and tired of wearing these extreme uniforms to school. Let's go help the guys."

"If they think they can kiss tulips, just watch us!" giggled Jacqui.

So, the two joined the rest of the friends to spread the dark-purple tulips.

A blast of wind spread the petals farther and farther into the country each time, as more and more six-petal, dark-purple tulips multiplied throughout the meadow.

The Uniformity Police were pinned behind the crowd, who now turned to watch the spectacle, cheering the teens who dared to spread the dark-purple tulips. Masuiah called the police together and redirected them around the crowd to the rear edge of the meadow.

"Take the road and drive off everyone who is standing there!" he ordered. "We'll circle to the back and set the meadow on fire. That will take care of these ignorant bumpkins. One of you ride back to Amudia and bring out my troops. I'll shape up this crowd and restore order."

The police did as Masuiah commanded. They drove the crowd from the road and galloped furiously to the rear edge of the meadow.

But it was to no avail. Each time they struck a flame, the wind blew it out.

"Let's join the teens," said Marbo, one of the pilgrims who had come to Amudia. "Jiana, let go of the boy. We came on a pilgrimage to glimpse at The Great Mountain, now something even more marvelous is happening right before our eyes."

Jiana took a deep breath. Then, she released Wozner. "I'm in," she said, as she found her first dark-purple tulip.

The leading citizens of Amudia joined the teens, kissing the tulips, making wishes for good, and blowing on the petals. More and more petals floated in the air and danced in the wind. Again and again, a gust hurled petals across the countryside. The stream of dark-purple blossoms widened to become a river of tulips running through the land.

Bilnot and a contingent from the Royal Guild of Gardeners arrived, meeting Masuiah on the road.

"This is all your fault, Bilnot!" cried Masuiah. "How could you have betrayed me? I have bestowed the district Uniformity Award on you ten years in a row. Have you gone mad? Have you forsaken our pact when we entered this land? I'll see you punished for your crime."

Bilnot replied, "Masuiah, don't you see what is happening? Has your heart grown hard and withered, too? It is the hand of The Almighty at work! The Almighty cannot be confined to routine and repetition. We are reclaiming the meadows for The Almighty, like they were before we came here."

"You will pay for this treason!" shouted Masuiah, shaking his white-gloved fist. He wheeled his horse toward Bilnot. "I will take care of you myself."

Masuiah charged toward Bilnot, but the Royal Guild formed a circle around him, raising their hoes and rakes in defense.

The Chancellor halted. There was no one to stand with him. The Uniformity Police were scattered throughout the meadow, chasing those spreading the dark-purple tulip petals. It was such a sight—grown men in uniform tumbling and stumbling, trying to prevent the purple petals from landing.

All of the townspeople were laughing at them.

Masuiah's face became a mask of fury. "Remember, I am the only one in Neer'stazone who can approach the Throne of The Almighty from the Great Mountain!" he shouted. "I'll return there now and you will regret the day you betrayed me!"

He whirled his horse around and galloped away toward Amudia.

"We have work to do," Bilnot addressed the other gardeners.

He took the pack from his back, opened it in front of them, and poured the contents onto the ground. Hundreds of seeds and bulbs glistened in the sunlight. One by one, the other gardeners stepped forward and scooped up handfuls of seeds.

"To the meadows of Neer'stazone!" they cried as each one set out to plant those seeds in whatever meadows they could reach.

Masuiah arrived in Amudia at sunset and rode directly to the Court of Uniformity. He jumped off his horse, entered the Court, and ran through the inner chambers to the purple door.

"I'll show Bilnot!" he muttered. "I will approach the Throne of The Almighty and end this episode immediately. The Scroll! I must pray the words on that Scroll!"

He fumbled under his tunic and brought out his purple and white amulet. He jiggled the amulet against the door to open it, but behold, the slot was gone! There was no opening in the purple door—it was sealed.

"NOOOOOOOO!" wailed the Chancellor, but it was no use. The purple door would never again be opened. The night was falling in Amudia and Neer'stazone.

Chapter Fourteen

At the Rainbow's End

The Plateau was lit with color as the Rainbow's End cascaded from high in the sky. The floor and walls of the Plateau reflected its light. At the left side of the Rainbow's End, a small stream of water flowed toward the mountainside, forming the waterfall Wilby had seen at the mountaintop. Wilby stepped down and started walking directly toward the spot where the Rainbow's End touched the Plateau. As she approached, a groan came from the rocks, and a shining being flew in front of the Rainbow's End. The being looked like a person, only there were no solid features, just dazzling rays of the six colors.

Wilby froze.

"Who *are* you?" called Wilby, shivering with fear.

"Who are *you*?" replied the radiant figure.

"I am Wilby of Eregon. I have come on a quest to bring the Rainbow's End back to my people. But *who* are you?"

"I am the Guardian Angel of Colors," stated the radiant figure. "Only The Almighty can pronounce my name, since it came from The Almighty."

"May I pass, please, to enter the Rainbow's End and direct it to my people?" asked Wilby.

"Wilby, you are on holy ground. Once before did someone dare to enter the Rainbow's End by trampling on holy ground," replied the Angel. "Invading holy ground had consequences. It caused a great division in the land. The Almighty created me to be its Guardian until the one came who would restore the land."

Wilby was overcome by the magnificence of the Angel's appearance and the authority of its words.

"I don't know what you mean by 'unite the land,'" she said. "I'm on a simple mission to ask The Almighty to bless my people."

"Is that truly your intention?" replied the Angel.

"Why, yes. I've journeyed for such a long time and thought of this moment so often. What else could I do?"

"What else?" asked the Angel. "What about riches? Don't you think that if you had access to the Throne of The Almighty that you could ask for whatever you wanted and then have immense riches? Think of where you came from. Your family is poor. Your land is bleak. Riches would provide an easy life for you. Aren't you really seeking riches?"

"I'm not here for riches," stated Wilby. "I want my people to experience the blessing of The Almighty. All of my people."

"What about power?" replied the Angel. "Don't you want the power that comes with speaking directly to The Almighty? Only the one who enters the Rainbow's End can touch and influence the Throne of The Almighty. With that kind of power, you can control people and events. They would do what *you* command. Aren't you really seeking power?"

"I don't want power for myself," said Wilby. "I want my people to share in the blessing of The Almighty, just like Neer'stazone has."

"Well, then. Aren't you really after fame? Don't you really want people to admire you, even worship you?" asked the Angel. "Why, if you could reach the ear of The Almighty, maybe you might think that you could even sit on The Almighty's Throne and be held in as high regard as The Almighty. Let me show you the Throne of The Almighty."

In an instant, Wilby and the Angel were at the other end of the Rainbow. There was a Throne set up like nothing ever seen in the land. From it, there gleamed a Presence more remarkable than all things that emit light, more brilliant than the sun, stars, fire, and lightning put together.

There was sound more magnificent than music, more astounding than thunder, grander than anything Wilby had ever heard or imagined.

The Throne rested on all types of precious stones. Its base was liquid-yet-solid amethyst, a purple foundation that rippled and danced like the waves in the Great River. The word *PEACE* flowed back and forth on this amethyst foundation.

Wilby shuddered and cringed at the sight. Waves of delight and ecstasy swept through her. She could not speak and became transfixed at the vision. In that instant, Wilby's white amulet shone with a radiance that reflected the glory of the One on the Throne.

In that instant, she was fully known, and she knew herself more clearly than at any other time in her entire life. She knew herself with a name that no one else could know or understand. There were no more questions, only a fullness of knowing deep and perfect *Love*. There seemed to be millions of people and beings in the Presence of the One on the Throne.

"My dream! The one I told Gramma. It's really coming true!" gasped Wilby.

"That's enough for now," cried the Angel. Suddenly, they were back on the Plateau. "Aren't you really seeking this glory? The blessing of The Almighty's glory?"

"No, no! NO! I'm not seeking glory! Not for myself. I just want people everywhere to have what I've seen. To live for peace, to be one, just like the land is one."

"Then you are ready," replied the Angel. "Come and enter. Deep and perfect love awaits you."

The Angel rose above the Plateau, hovered for a moment, flashed into a brilliant white light, and vanished. Wilby was left standing alone.

Now is the time; this is the moment.

Wilby approached the Rainbow's End, and It started to throb with light and color. Wilby tried to focus her thoughts.

Think of our land; return the Rainbow's End to our land. Think of our land; return the Rainbow's End to our land. Think of our land; return the Rainbow's End to our land. The King's words echoed in her mind.

Wilby narrowed her eyes and tried to visualize Hdora, Gramma, her friends, the land, and the King's Fortress.

The more Wilby tried to think of these things, the more a litany of other images, names, and voices came to mind. *Kellin, Wozner, Lady Trentum and Trentum the Great. Jahaamaa. Bilnot, the gardener. Umdai and the children of Neer'stazone. The mountain.*

No boundaries. The Governor. Friends here, all the same. What will become of their land without the Rainbow's End?

Wilby stood within arm's length of the Rainbow's End and stretched out her right hand toward its rays. As the Rainbow's light danced on Wilby's fingers, so too did the last color on the amulet, purple, appear.

Wilby's amulet now glowed with a flashing, full-color image of the Rainbow's End. A rumble deep from within the land sounded, and the Plateau shook. Wilby was whisked by a mighty wind into the center of the Rainbow's End.

For a moment, the Rainbow's End shuddered. Then, an earthquake rocked the Plateau. With a flash of lightning and a crash of thunder, the Rainbow's End was ripped from the Plateau. A large gray cloud descended from the sky, slowly removing the Rainbow from above. Soon, all traces of the Rainbow's colors had disappeared, leaving only a gray veil covering the blue sky. Wilby had disappeared, too! Her amulet fell into the stream and hurtled over the edge of the Plateau.

"It's gone! It's gone!" shouted the Seer. "I can't believe she's done this!"

He stormed into the Greeting Room of the King. The King was stooped on the carved, wooden Throne, half-thinking, half-sleeping. The Seer marched up to the Throne and bowed, "Sire, the Rainbow's End is gone!"

"What?!!" said the King. "Well, that means Wilby was successful. She did it! We should be seeing the Rainbow's End coming here soon. Shouldn't we?"

The Seer stared angrily at the King, "You don't understand, do you? Didn't you feel the tremor in the land this morning? It is not a good sign."

"Seer, I really wonder about you at times. You know that we picked Wilby because of her virtue. She wouldn't steal the Rainbow's End. If she did, where would she take it? Where else could the Rainbow's End have gone? There are only two kingdoms, and if it's gone from Neer'stazone, it must be coming here."

"No! Wilby has *failed*. It's all messed up!"

"You're talking gibberish. Calm down and explain yourself!" replied the King.

"Look! Look out your tower window," the Seer exclaimed as he rushed to the shutter and flung it open. "See, the gray clouds are gathering. The *gray veil* clouds. Don't you remember the *gray veil?*"

The King became pale and sunk into his Throne, "You don't mean—"

"Yes! Yes, that's exactly what I mean. The Rainbow's End is no more!"

"How could she have failed at this?" uttered the King. "Weren't you the one who picked her for this mission? Didn't you read it in the Scrolls?"

The Seer winced. "I should have known better, really, I should I have known better. She is just like her father... and your brother!"

The King sprang from the Throne. "My brother, her father—and yes, your apprentice! Masuiah, your apprentice, *your son*, was the ringleader of the three who stole the Rainbow's End in the first place. He learned all about it from you. He *trampled* on holy ground! And now, you're blaming Wilby?"

The Seer hung his head and whispered, "There still may be a way." He turned abruptly and staggered out of the throne room just as furiously as he had entered.

Rosalina stood at the door as the Seer passed by. The King saw her and invited her in. She strode into the Throne Room, her face set with determination.

"So, the Rainbow's End has left again!" she declared. "Where in the land is my granddaughter now?"

"I don't know," replied the King. "We can only pray that she is within the protection of The Almighty."

"Before Wilby left Hdora, I asked your men if my granddaughter would be taken away like her father was. And now it's happened. No more Rainbow's End, anywhere. You sent no one with her. What do you think your brother and Masuiah will do to her?"

"My brother . . . well, my brother will probably declare war." The King sighed and shook his head. "He always was like that: the first to fight; the first to take. At least we're separated and shielded by the Great River, which is impossible to cross. And Masuiah, if he finds Wilby, he'll. . . he'll try her and punish her. I am so very sorry at this turn of events, Rosalina."

"No more sorry than I am," Rosalina broke down and sobbed. "What could be coming next?" The King put his arm around her shoulder.

"We still have hope," he whispered. "There is still a chance for your son to help us."

The sky of Neer'stazone did indeed turn gray. There were no patches of blue, no rays of sunshine anywhere. The landscape changed overnight from a lush garden full of trees, bushes, and flowers into a dry, desolate place like Eregon had become.

The source of water that flowed from the Rainbow's End at the Great Mountain was no more. The waterfall stopped flowing, and the underground springs that fed the meadows and forests were no more. The stream of Neer'stazone that fed the Great River receded to a ribbon of muddy sludge in the middle of the streambed.

The five-petal flowers in the meadows began to droop, turn brown, and wither. Yet the seeds and bulbs that Bilnot and the Royal Guild of Gardeners had planted began to thrive, drawing moisture and life-force from the dark-purple tulips.

Masuiah's police still pursued those spreading the petals of the dark-purple tulips, which remained in bloom. More and more citizens of Neer'stazone kissed the tulips, made good wishes and blew on the petals. The dark-purple tulips grew throughout the muddy streambed, as the wind blew them furiously toward the Great River.

It was a peculiar sight, citizens standing on the shore of the stream, kissing the dark-purple petals into the streambed, and Masuiah's once fastidiously dressed troops covered with mud, diving to prevent the petals from landing.

The wall of water in the middle of the Great River fell with a loud splash and was no more. In fact, the Great River itself began to shrink and dry up; the springs that fed it disappeared.

The army of Eregon put all of its troops on the shore, frantically sweeping water toward the water drawing plant so that there would be enough water to distribute to the residents of each land. If this weren't enough, a gale began to sweep over the face of the Great River, hastening its evaporation.

The Great River had become a large, muddy field within a short time. Once the dark-purple tulips had sprouted in the streambed, they multiplied rapidly. They radiated like a blanket across the large muddy field that had been the Great River.

Part of Neer'stazone's army wallowed through that mud, trying to stop the flow of the dark-purple tulips. But it was no use. The tulips completely covered the riverbed and expanded down the road winding through the borderlands of Eregon.

The river of dark purple twisted through the borderland's black rocks and brown soil until the flowers surrounded the Plateau where the Rainbow's End had once touched Eregon. Then the wind ceased blowing, and the tulips stopped spreading.

Bilnot had organized the Royal Guild of Gardeners to help spread the tulips. A gardener approached him, holding a muddy object swinging from a gold chain.

"What is that?" Bilnot asked.

"I don't know, but I found it in the river bed when we were marching through it to plant the seeds and bulbs you gave us," the gardener replied.

"Let me see it." Bilnot wiped the mud from the object and washed it with water from his canteen.

"It looks like an amulet, of some type," he said. "It's white with an image of the Rainbow's End on it. I've seen this somewhere before. But where?"

He turned the amulet over, paused, and then remembered. "This amulet was worn by the girl in the meadow! I remember that it fell loose from her shirt when she visited my meadow. But it's changed somehow; the colors are reversed! The color red is on top; the color purple is on the bottom."

Purple must now replace red. The thought shot into Bilnot's mind like a flash of light. *Free Kellin. Use the amulet to free Kellin.*

"I must find Kellin!" Bilnot exclaimed. "Where is she?"

"She's caged in the marketplace of the Palace City," replied the gardener.

Bilnot raced to the Palace City. The streets were deserted, and the market was abandoned. Kellin lay in the iron cage as if in a coma. Her daughter, Umdai, sat on the ground crying. Bilnot rushed to the door and banged on it.

"Who are you?" sniffled Umdai.

"Oh, how can I open the cage?" he cried.

Use the amulet to free Kellin.

Bilnot saw the slot on the cage door and shoved the amulet into the slot. The door swung open.

"Kellin! Kellin!" shouted Bilnot. "Where are you!"

He and Umdai ripped the piles of petals from the cage and uncovered Kellin. Her body was stiff and still. Bilnot knelt beside her. A tear fell on her cheek as he kissed it.

Then, Kellin work up. "Wh...where am I?' she asked.

"You're safe now," Bilnot whispered.

"Oh, Mom!" cried Umdai. "Oh, Mom!"

"How did you open that door?" Kellin muttered weakly. "Only Masuiah's amulet could unlock the cage."

"I found a white amulet with a rainbow on it," replied Bilnot, "and a thought kept coming to me to use it to free you. When I learned you were here, I came."

"Why, that is Wilby's amulet!" gasped Kellin. "It's Wilby's white amulet."

"Wilby again! Just who is this Wilby that crosses my path?" asked Bilnot.

"Wake up, Bilnot!" Kellin rasped. "She is your *daughter!*"

"Wilby, my Wilby, my daughter? My little tulip?" asked Bilnot, his heart now fully soft. "How could I have forgotten about my little tulip?"

"The Chancellor is a master of mesmerizing and manipulating."

"His daughter?" asked Umdai. "Where are they from?"

Just then, the captain of the Royal Guard saw the open cage and charged toward them.

"Let's go!" Bilnot yelled as he hoisted both Kellin and Umdai upon his horse.

They galloped down Main Street and out of the city toward the riverbed. The captain, who was on foot, stopped his pursuit. He returned to the marketplace and examined the door of the cage. He pulled Wilby's amulet out of the door and stuffed it under his belt.

Chapter Fifteen
A War Over the Flowers

When Masuiah and the Captains of the Uniformity Police received reports of all that went on, they became even more furious. Masuiah and his police converged on the Palace City, seeking to overthrow the Governor of Neer'stazone and restore order. General Neber approached the Governor, who had locked himself inside the Throne Room of the Palace City.

"Your excellency," called the General. "Your excellency, you must see this!"

"What is it?" the Governor replied.

"Kellin has been freed. The Captain of your Royal Guard found this in the door of the cage in our marketplace. Do you recognize it?"

The General held out Wilby's white amulet that now displayed a gleaming image of the Rainbow's End on it. The colors were arranged in neat, curved lines, but something was different. Red was on top, with orange, yellow, green, and blue beneath it. Purple was on the bottom.

The Governor grasped the rim of the white amulet and examined it. *Someone made it into the Rainbow's End! That is something that we failed to do.*

"This is treason!" cried the Governor. "This is the work of a spy! A spy from Eregon!"

"From Eregon, Sire?" replied the General. "Why, Eregon is such a—"

The Governor shot back. "Don't underestimate the cunning of Eregon. Someone came from Eregon to steal the Rainbow's End. Quickly, we must get the Rainbow's End back. Summon the troops! And bring that amulet!"

No sooner had the Governor left the Throne Room than Masuiah marched into the Palace with the Captains of his Uniformity Police. The Royal Guards intercepted them and summoned General Neber to the site.

"Ah, Chancellor Masuiah!" said the General. "What brings you to the Palace today?"

"Stop the pleasantries, Neber!" replied Masuiah. "I need to see the Governor! Now!"

"What do you want from me, Masuiah?" asked the Governor, who had entered the Majestic Hall. "Are you here to tell me that the Rainbow's End is gone?"

"How did *you* know?" exclaimed Masuiah.

Signaling to General Neber, the Governor retrieved the white amulet. He took Masuiah aside and showed it to him. "Doesn't this look familiar?"

Masuiah grabbed the amulet and inspected the image of the Rainbow's End. "The color purple has moved; it's no longer at the top!" he declared. "It's at the bottom." the Governor replied.

"How did you get this?"

"A patrol found it in the door of the cage where you locked Kellin."

"Kellin is free?" replied Masuiah. "Only my amulet could open that cage. Only my amulet could open the purple door leading to the Great Mountain. Now the cage is open and the purple door is sealed."

"You know what this means, don't you?"

"There was another amulet! The Seer must have hidden it from us," snarled Masuiah. "I took the Seer's amulet. Someone came from Eregon with another amulet. But who?"

"Who would the King pick to avenge her father?" The Governor raised an eyebrow.

"It must be Bilnot's daughter!" returned Masuiah. "But she was only a child when it happened. The three of us—Bilnot, you, and I—surrounded the Rainbow's End in Eregon. We knew its secrets. I had stolen the words of the Scroll from my father. We thought that we could control the whims of The Almighty, have actual contact with the Throne of The Almighty. We were within inches, *inches*, of entering the Rainbow's End."

"You did succeed, Masuiah," replied the Governor. "You touched it. But only your fingers actually entered the purple, the highest and outermost color. You were the only one of us to make contact with the Rainbow's End."

"I remember only too well!" Masuiah tore the white glove from his right hand and held up his withered palm and fingers.

"This is what touching the purple color of the Rainbow's End did to me!" raged Masuiah. "It destroyed my hand. Do you think that The Almighty loved me to have the Rainbow's End do this to me? Wasn't the Throne of The Almighty at the other end of the Rainbow? It was written in the Scrolls; my father, the Seer, told me so. I ripped that part of the Scroll and took the amulet from the purple box. I proclaimed the sacred words at the Rainbow's End just before I entered, just like my father did!"

The Governor interrupted him, "Well, your father never moved the Rainbow's End from Eregon, did he? *Your* plan backfired. You recruited me, and we recruited Bilnot, the best gardener in Eregon, to join us. We promised him a life of riches, power, and fame. We all sought those things. When we failed to enter the Rainbow's End, it disappeared, the gray clouds gathered in Eregon, and the land turned brown. The rain stopped, the flowers wilted, and the crops died. The King learned about our actions and hunted us."

"That's something I don't want to remember," replied Masuiah.

"We fled to the west and built Amudia," continued the Governor. "The Rainbow's End moved, too, and the Great River came into being. We made a pact never to return. You created the Code of Uniformity and excluded purple from any appearance in Neer'stazone. Well now, look what's popping up all over in Neer'stazone: dark-purple tulips."

Masuiah stared at the Governor for a long time.

Finally, he said: *"What is alike is one. How good it is. What is one is good and pleasing to The Almighty.* The Code of Uniformity is Supreme. Bilnot has betrayed us. Bilnot's daughter has betrayed us. They have polluted Neer'stazone with the ways of Eregon. We have no choice but to declare war on Eregon. *They* have destroyed the Rainbow's End. They have damaged *our* land, transgressed *our* meadows, and frightened *our* people. Why are we wasting our time standing here? We should be marching to war!"

"This is like old times, isn't it?" The Governor smiled. "We can still control our destiny and the land. We'll show the King that *we* are still in charge. General Neber!"

The General ran from the adjacent chamber. "Yes, your Honor!" he said, saluting.

"Gather the army; we are going to war!"

And so, the land of Neer'stazone alerted the rest of its troops and army. So large was their number that the soil shook as they marched toward Eregon. The sound of their stomping was echoed by rumbling in the gray clouds above their heads.

The lookout in the Fortress Tower of Eregon caught sight of the dust clouds and heard the sound of marching. He ran to the Throne Room to rouse the King with the news.

"Sire! Sire! The armies of Neer'stazone are coming!" Panting, he led the King to the Tower window to witness the approaching throng.

"Call the Palace Guard!" exclaimed the King. "Assemble our army, our patrols, our citizens! We must go to battle and defend ourselves."

Likewise, the entire army of Eregon, its officers, patrols, and soldiers convened and marched toward Neer'stazone. Both armies advanced to the borderlands of Eregon. They entered each end of the twisting road that led to the Plateau where the Rainbow's End had once touched the land of Eregon. When they reached the opposite ends of the Plateau, both armies stopped and set up camp. Night fell, and the air surrounding them became utterly still.

At daybreak, a lone rider seated on a bright white horse galloped toward the Plateau. The horse was more brilliant than any other horse in the land. It seemed to float above the ground, as one might see in a dream. When the rider arrived, she dismounted, walked across the Plateau, and stood near the great fissure in the rock. It was Wilby.

News of Wilby's arrival spread through both camps as quickly as the dark-purple tulips had spread from Neer'stazone to Eregon. When the King, the Seer, and the Governor learned of this, they called a truce and met her on the Plateau. But the Chancellor Masuiah was nowhere to be found.

The only remaining ray of sunlight pierced the clouds and fell on the large jagged rift in the black rock. Attendants set up an open tent supported by four wooden poles. The top of the tent was striped canvas, which fluttered freely in the breeze.

Wilby was dressed in a dazzling white robe. Above Wilby's right eye was the mark of the Rainbow. All the colors were there: red on top, followed by orange, yellow, green, and blue. The color purple was on the bottom. Wilby's skin was brighter than anyone had seen before; it almost seemed to glow like the glory of lilies awash in sunbeams. The King, the Governor, and the Seer were dumbfounded at Wilby's appearance. They began to ask her many questions.

"Where have you been?" asked the King.

"What's happened to your face?" asked the Seer.

"Why did you betray the Order of Friendship that I gave you?" asked the Governor.

"WHERE IS THE RAINBOW'S END??" all three shouted at her.

"You've coveted the Rainbow's End because you believed it was connected to the Throne of The Almighty and that It alone brought blessing to your land," Wilby began. "Yes, I've seen the Middle of the Rainbow, which encircles The Almighty's Throne. But the Rainbow is not The Almighty; it is only a messenger."

"You've seen it—the Throne of The Almighty?" gasped the King. "And you're still alive?"

"Yes, I'm still alive," said Wilby. "In fact, I seem to be more alive than ever before."

"But the colors of the Rainbow's End on your face—they are flipped upside down! Purple, the color closest to The Almighty, is no longer on top, the closest to the heavens," exclaimed the Seer.

"Are you saying that The Almighty doesn't live up in the heavens?" asked the King.

"Do we have an Almighty who is fickle and likes to change what has been established? Is the color red now more important than purple? Explain that!" demanded the Governor.

"Friend Governor, the color purple is still closest to The Almighty," explained Wilby. "But you see, the Throne of The Almighty is not just high up in the sky; the Presence of The Almighty is right here, among us. It is such a twist; no one place can contain The Almighty, yet the Throne of The Almighty dwells within us. Therefore, the color purple is closest to us, too."

"You're bordering on heresy, Wilby!" exclaimed the Seer.

"We carry the Rainbow within us," Wilby repeated. "It is within us that the Throne of The Almighty dwells. Sometimes it bursts through to the outside, to mark our appearance, like the image over my eye. Many times, especially on dark days, the

Rainbow is only seen through actions such as the kind deeds we do for each other or the ways that we show love to each other. We need to see the Rainbow within us and let it out. Then, the holy ground will be in our lives."

"Humpph!" grunted the King. "When we sent you on the mission to bring back the Rainbow's End to our land, you had no knowledge of what it even was! Now, look at you. You're preaching to us!"

"Wilby, you've always asked such good questions," said the Seer. "Let me ask you a few questions since you were at the Throne of the Almighty. Why did The Almighty allow my son to enter the Rainbow's End with bad intentions? Why did the Rainbow's End leave Eregon?"

"Why did the Rainbow's End go to Neer'stazone?" asked the King.

"Why was the land troubled with famine and drought? Why did all of the flowers disappear? Why did the grey veil cover the sky and hide the sun for so many years?" added the Seer.

Wilby breathed deeply. "I don't know why. I've wondered about them myself."

"But you saw the Throne of The Almighty," said the King. "Didn't you ask The Almighty these questions?"

"Yes, I saw The Almighty's Throne and it was beyond anything I could ever know," replied Wilby. "I was so overcome with awe, I didn't think to ask those questions. Perhaps The Almighty will answer in the Almighty's own time."

"The Almighty's own time," sighed the Seer. "Yes, The Almighty has reasons and time known only to The Almighty. Even though we've had a long time of famine, we survived. We learned new things. We learned to scriggle for life. We learned to harvest food and water wisely, how to persevere in difficult times, how not to lose hope, and to hold on to the hope that The Almighty would work things out for our good."

"The Almighty did form the Great River to provide water for the land and the people, even after the Rainbow left and the waterfall fell," added the King.

"Perhaps there is more good to come," said Wilby. "Perhaps The Almighty allowed these things to happen because there are even better things in store for us."

"Your majesty, you did ask that Wilby be guided by the breath of The Almighty, didn't you?" asked the Seer.

"Well, our prayers to The Almighty never imagined an outcome like this!" The King sighed heavily.

"Just what did you pray for?" asked the Governor. "That only your side of the land would be blessed? Look at it now. Is there anything in the land that is not cursed? Only these purple tulips are everywhere. What a turn of events! If purple *is* the sign of The Almighty's presence, it can never be excluded."

"In the Kingdom before Eregon, we had never excluded the color purple," explained the King. "It was as present among us as was any color. Don't you remember those times? Why did you exclude purple in Neer'stazone?"

"Why did we exclude purple?" echoed the Governor. "Because Masuiah demanded it when he became Chancellor."

"That became *real* trouble, which started when my son trampled on holy ground," sighed the Seer.

Chapter Sixteen

The Return of the Rainbow

The King's army found Chancellor Masuiah and brought him forward at the Plateau. With all of the people assembled, the Seer began the trial of Masuiah, his son.

The court convened, and the charge was brought forward of spreading a false doctrine of uniformity, based on a mistranslation of a small fragment of one of the Sacred Scrolls.

The Seer began this testimony. "My son, when you took the purple amulet to enter the Rainbow's End for your own selfish purposes, you trampled on holy ground. The consequences of that action divided the Kingdom and separated the people. The Scroll you took and used to create the Code of Uniformity is a fragment of the collection of Scrolls kept in the King's Fortress. You have said, 'What is alike is one. How good it is. What is one is good, and pleasing to The Almighty.'"

"The text of the Scroll that includes the fragment actually is *'How good it is, and pleasing to The Almighty, when all are one though many.'*"

"You have misinterpreted, misread, and misspelled the text, the scroll, and its meaning! Look at what you have done to thousands of people—the many who are one! The Scrolls call for unity, not uniformity. You have forced all the people of Neer'stazone and all of creation to look alike, to speak alike, and to behave alike. This is a grave crime, a great sin to the Throne of The Almighty."

A loud murmur ran through the vast crowd when they heard the Seer's words. Neer'stazone's officers and soldiers were pierced with a wound much deeper and sharper than any weapon could inflict. Tears streaked down the cheeks of the Uniformity Police, for they realized their life's work had been in vain. The many citizens who decorated their homes and workplaces with garlands of five-petal flowers became downcast.

"What shall be done with Masuiah and us?" General Neber, the leader of Neer'stazone's army cried. "Shall we punish him? He has violated the Scrolls and the Throne of The Almighty."

"Yes! Yes!" cried the crowd. "Masuiah is guilty. He is the one who has betrayed us all! He is not fit to live."

When Masuiah heard this, he became pale and weak. "I have done wrong, my father," he whimpered. "I have done wrong. Will you forgive me for what I have done?"

"Forgive him? FORGIVE HIM?" shouted the Governor. "Are you crazy? After all that he has done? He must be punished. An example must be made! People of Neer'stazone, shall Masuiah not pay for his crimes?"

The people of Neer'stazone became enraged at Masuiah. "Punish him! Punish him!" they all cried in a fever pitch.

The Seer raised his staff and looked at the people. One by one, they became quiet until silence enfolded the entire Plateau.

"There is a very old scroll, which we must take seriously, especially now," the Seer. "The words go something like this:

> "As I live, says The Almighty, I take no pleasure in the death of those who do wrong, but rather that they turn away from doing wrong to do right, that all My people may live."

"I forgot about that verse," added the King.

"I had never heard that one before," the Governor murmured. "General Neber, we must honor the words of The Almighty. Masuiah, do you really want to change?"

"Yes, I commit to honoring The Almighty and all people. No more 'Five Fingers, Five Toes.' No more five petals or five colors only. No more Code of Uniformity that destroys unity."

"Then, my son, I forgive you," the Seer said as a tear ran down his cheek into his beard. "The past cannot be changed. All the wrong that has been done is done. We will not repeat that wrong now. You cannot repeat what you have done. You must pledge to restore the land. The present must change so that the future will bring a new day."

"I do pledge to restore the land," muttered Masuiah. "Can a new day *really* come, my father?"

"Do you have the white amulet, the one I gave to Wilby?" the Seer asked. "Bring it to me."

Masuiah reached beneath his tunic and drew out Wilby's white amulet that still glowed with the image of the Rainbow's End. He gave the amulet to the Seer, who held it above his head.

"Take off the white glove and stretch out your hand," the Seer commanded. "Touch the amulet with it."

Masuiah removed the white glove from his withered right hand. He looked at his hand and sobbed, "What have I done?" Then, he stretched his hand over his head and touched the amulet.

The Seer cried out, "Let all in the valley and in the heights and on the Plateau call upon the Almighty's Throne. Let us beseech The Almighty for mercy for Masuiah—and for us."

There was a rustle in the crowd as someone slipped forward and stood before the Seer. It was Kellin. Umdai stood next to her.

"I, too, will pray for Masuiah," Kellin said, placing her hand on his shoulder, as she held Umdai's hand.

"You would pray for Masuiah, Kellin?" Bilnot shouted from the crowd. "He locked you in a cage! Why would you pray for Masuiah?"

"He is living in his own cage," replied Kellin. "He, too, must be set free."

There was more rustling in the crowd. "Me, too!" shouted Wozner as he ran forward. "Come on, Jahaamaa!"

Jahaamaa came forward and touched his uncle's sleeve. "This is such a turn of events, Uncle," he whispered. "Yes, of course, it's a twist. We are praying for you now. Before, you alone prayed for Neer'stazone."

Masuiah looked at Jahaamaa with tears in his eyes. "I've treated you so poorly," he said. "Could you ever forgive me?"

"Of course, I forgive you, Uncle." Jahaamaa leaned over and kissed his cheek.

Wilby and her companions, all came forward and formed a circle around them. The people, too, became still, held hands, and bowed their heads.

"Let everyone raise their joined hands and unite with me as we pray," the Seer continued. He closed his eyes and whispered, "Come, O Breath of The Almighty that circles the land and returns to The Almighty's Throne. Come, restore life and health to us. Blow your love into our hearts and your peace into our minds. How good it is, and pleasing to The Almighty, when all are one though many."

Then, it began to rain for the first time in many years.

At first, a sprinkle.

Then, a steady downpour. The people were drenched with rain.

"It's raining! It's raining!!" cried Lemet. "We can go home now."

"This is what rain is, Mom?" Umdai said to Kellin.

"Yes, this is rain, water from the heavens to grow the flowers and bring us back to The Almighty," Kellin replied.

Then, the rain stopped.

At once, a shrill, whistling sound emanated from the dark fissure in the wall of rock above them. The noise increased to a deafening pitch. Suddenly, a geyser of air gushed forth from the fissure. It circled the Seer, Masuiah, and all gathered around them like a driving wind. The flesh of Masuiah's fingers began to glow, too, as a shaft of white light flashed from the amulet. Within moments, his hand became fully restored.

Then, the geyser of wind pushed toward the sky and pierced the gray veil covering the sky above the Plateau. The people of

Eregon looked up and saw the sun shining for the first time in many years.

"Glory to The Almighty!" they shouted in amazement. The gray veil dissolved, and the sky became clear blue. As they were looking, the Rainbow's End descended toward the Plateau like a waterfall from the sky.

And behold! The colors of the Rainbow's End had reversed their order: red was now the highest color, then orange, yellow, green, blue, and purple. Purple was now the closest color to the people and the land. The colors of the Rainbow's End danced upon the deep fissure in the rock above the Plateau. A new waterfall burst down the side of the cliff. At long last, flowing water had returned to the land of Eregon.

As the people gazed at the sight, the colors of the Rainbow's End stretched away from the middle of the sky toward the land of Neer'stazone. The other End of the Rainbow dropped from the sky toward the Great Mountain and rested on the Plateau there, restoring that waterfall. Thus, the Rainbow touched both ends of the land, east and west, Eregon, and Neer'stazone, making them one.

"What does this mean?" asked the King. "Have the prophecies of the Scrolls finally come to pass?"

"Yes. We have become united!" beamed the Seer. "We have witnessed the work of The Almighty."

"Isn't it amazing, how it all worked out?" said the Governor.

"In what way, brother?" replied the King.

"The work of the Almighty. It's like nothing that we could have imagined, planned, or done. I'm sorry we split ways so long ago, Luda. I am at fault for that."

"I forgive you, Pemer," said King Luda. We are brothers and family back together again, in a stronger way. I am grateful for that."

"What have we learned from all of this?" asked Wilby.

"Perhaps, we can pray to The Almighty, just where we are, and not by entering The Rainbow's End," added Rosalina.

"Perhaps, all of us can pray, use scriggle, and have hope," said Umdai.

"Now, the Great River has dried up and there are no more barriers to separate us," observed King Luda. "Maybe we are ready to be friends again."

"Shall we still have two different names for our one land?" asked Governor Pemer.

"No, we should have one name," responded King Luda. "We have one land, yes? But what shall we call it?"

"We could try combining the names," piped in Lemet. "Maybe, instead of Eregon, we could have *Neer'gon*? Or instead of Neer'stazone, we might call the land *Erstazone?*

"Lemet is always speaking his mind," said Cargas. "I'm sorry I haven't always listened to him."

"I like them both," said King Luda and Governor Pemer at the same time. "Which one shall we choose?"

Bilnot said, "Why not ask the people? Should they not have a say in this?"

"Excellent, Bilnot!" they said in unison. "Lemet, Cargas, Neber, assemble your troops and find out what the people want to be called." And so a vote was taken among all the people who assembled on the Plateau and throughout the land. It took some time, as such things often do, but after everyone cast a vote, the name *Neer'gon* was chosen.

Bilnot approached the King and the Governor, "Sires, please pardon my question. What shall we do about who leads these vast people who now are united in one land named *Neer'gon*?"

"Excuse us, Bilnot," said Governor Pemer. The two rulers walked about one hundred feet away and began talking to each other. They laughed and, several minutes later, came walking back, arm-in-arm.

"Well, who is the new leader?" cried Lemet.

"You say this, my brother," said King Luda to Governor Pemer.

"Gladly, Luda. We have decided that it is time for a Council of people, young and old, rich and poor, women and men, to govern these vast people," pronounced the King. "We will have a Council of people who are open to the voice of The Almighty, so that the Throne of The Almighty may always be with us."

"I must return to the Throne of The Almighty," said Wilby. "It is my destiny to dwell there forever."

She approached the Rainbow's End and was about to enter when Jahaamaa ran forward and fell on his knees.

"Will you please stay, Wilby?" he pleaded. "Please stay with us. You've said that the Throne of The Almighty is within us. Won't you stay with us?"

"Yes, Wilby," interrupted the Seer, "you must stay here and help lead the people. You must replace me. You must live here to remind everyone that the Throne of The Almighty dwells in our hearts and in our land. Your destiny is to be with your people."

Bilnot stepped forward at the edge of the crowd. Rosalina, who had camped near the King's tent, spotted Bilnot and ran toward him. She threw her arms around Bilnot and cried, "My son, my long-lost son!" They wept together, and the sound of their joy filled the Plateau.

Sobbing, Bilnot stretched out his arms to Wilby, "Wilby! Wilby, my daughter, I love you – my little tulip. It has been so long ... " His voice broke off. "You are home now. Please stay with us."

Wilby turned away from the Rainbow's End and ran toward her father. "Dad!" she shouted as she flung her arms around him. "Yes, I am with you. I am home!"

Tears streaked down their faces as Rosalina, Bilnot, and Wilby embraced each other.

The entire crowd erupted in a cheer that resounded across the land.

One by one, the people of Neer'stazone turned to their long-lost kin of Eregon with words of forgiveness, welcome, and goodwill. There was great rejoicing in the reunion of that day that had never been seen before in the land.

Wozner spotted his brothers, Wil and Wes. "Hey, guys! Did you meet Jacqui and Carol? They helped us when we were kissing the tulips. Let me introduce you."

"It looks like Jahaamaa is already taken," Jacqui whispered to Carol. "Let's meet the boys."

And so, it came to be. King Luda and Governor Pemer returned to the Fortress City to rule together until the people elected a Council. The empty chairs at the long table in the Great Hall were filled with new, bright faces.

Kellin and Bilnot were chosen to be the Council co-moderators. The armies disbanded. The one Kingdom of Neer'gon was restored. Then the two rulers resigned, leaving the Council to govern the land. Wilby replaced the Seer and traveled throughout the land, reminding the people of The Almighty's presence in their midst. Umdai, Jahaamaa, and Wozner went with her. As time passed, Bilnot and Kellin became great friends and their love for each other blossomed. They opened a nursery, and their work became so blessed by The Almighty that people throughout Neer'gon came to buy seedlings there.

To keep Masuiah honest about his pledge, the Council sentenced him to peddle flower seeds for the rest of his life. He partnered with Bilnot and Kellin, and the land flourished with flowers of great beauty. Even the borderlands were transformed into a lush garden, and an abundance of peace filled the land.

WHAT'S COMING NEXT?

A Message from Dave

Dear Friend:

Thank you for reading *The Rainbow Chronicles: A Story of Hope for Today*. I hope you enjoyed this story of Wilby's journey to restore the Rainbow's End to her land. Through her deep and perfect love, she asked The Almighty to remove the trouble and bring peace through her prayers and actions.

While Wilby is the main character in this story, she didn't succeed by herself. She had the help of The Almighty, along with her friends, Wozner, Jahaamaa, and Umdai. They worked together with the adults in their lives: Gramma (Rosalina), Kellin, Bilnot, the King, and the Seer, among many others.

This story asks "What's coming next?" Trouble or peace? A desert or a garden?

WHAT'S COMING NEXT?

There is plenty of trouble in today's world. In the past two years alone, we've experienced the troubles of COVID-19, brokenness in families, increased crime, separation and division, abuse of all types, shootings, and murders, shortages, much higher prices, dramatic swings in the climate with wildfires and storms, a Russian invasion of Ukraine, and much more.

It's easy to let the bad news get you down so that you feel anxious and hopeless.

Yet, there is much good news that doesn't make the headlines on TV or on social media. There is plenty of hope available because God is always available. God is present. All. the. time.

The good news is that God works through people, like you and me. Hope grows when we plant seeds of peace. We do our best to love others and live at peace to keep trouble away. We pray and ask God to take care of the trouble that we can't.

The rainbow is a sign of hope. In the story of Noah in the Bible, God gave the rainbow to people in trouble. God promised a new beginning and to always be with creation.

Hundreds of years after the Flood, God kept that promise by sending Jesus on a mission to bring all people together, united in one Kingdom. God offers you the gift of the deep and perfect love of Jesus. Jesus lived, died, and rose to new life to show us God's deep and perfect *LOVE*. Jesus is still with us today and will be until the end of time. We are forever a family of God.

I believe that you can be like Wilby and her friends. I believe that God gives you a deep and perfect love to share with others on your life's journey. So how do you get through the twists and turns of your journey?

With a Hope Patch.

If you can, plant your own Hope Patch. Use a pot, a planter, or a patch of land. Plant some flower seeds and bulbs in the dirt. Water your Hope Patch. Watch the plants grow and the leaves unfold. Let the dazzling beauty of fragile flower petals amaze you. Kiss a tulip. Sniff a lilac bush.

Then, plant a seed of peace in your life today. Make hope come alive. It's okay to be soft-hearted. Start small. Make a wish and ask for something good to happen. Listen to the Holy Spirit. Smile and be kind. Say thank you and you're welcome. Compliment someone. Share a cookie or a piece of pound cake. Hold the door open for the person behind you. Say a prayer for someone who is in trouble. Give away something you don't use to someone who needs it. Scriggle when you meet obstacles. Forgive someone who hurt you. Do one thing to help someone today – and then do another one tomorrow.

Your prayers and actions can inspire someone else. Love and peace spread, like petals of the dark-purple tulips, to bring a future full of hope. God invites you to the Rainbow's End today and the rest of your life. It doesn't matter if you are tall or short, big or little, or anywhere in between. *You* can make a difference for good in your life and the lives of those you meet.

So, what is coming next? Trouble or peace? In many ways, it's up to you! May you help others find the Rainbow's End – hope, peace, and love – in their lives.

The peace of Jesus is with you.

Dave Pipitone, Easter 2022

P.S. If you have trouble experiencing peace, I invite you to listen to the prayer meditation, "Encountering Jesus in the Rainbow Garden." You can find this prayer at www.transforminglife-

WHAT'S COMING NEXT?

press.com/rainbowgarden. Feel free to share this prayer with others.

Feel free to connect with us on Facebook at: https://www.facebook.com/therainbowchroniclesstory

LIST OF CHARACTERS

- Bilnot – Chief Gardener in Neer'stazone
- Cargas – Captain of the King's Calvary in Eregon
- Chancellor Masuiah – The Chancellor of Neer'stazone, who wrote and enforced the Code of Uniformity
- Frivop – Captain in Neer'stazone's Uniformity Police
- Geka – Officer in charge of the Great River water drawing station in Eregon
- The Governor – Governs the land of Neer'stazone
- Jahaamaa – Fourteen-year-old boy, nephew of Chancellor Masuiah
- Kellin – Gardener in Neer'stazone's Guild, mother of Umdai, who grows the Hope Patch
- The King – Ruler of Eregon
- Lemet – Lieutenant in the King's Calvary and Wilby's guide
- Marbo, Jiana and Rogzy – Pilgrims to Amudia in Neer'stazone
- Neber – General of the Neer'stazone Army

LIST OF CHARACTERS

- Rucda – Gardener in the Guild of Neer'stazone
- Rosalina – Wilby's grandmother
- The Seer – Spiritual leader of Eregon
- Grand Viceroy Trentum – District magistrate from Nowlingburg in Neer'stazone
- Lady Trentum – Wife of the Grand Viceroy
- Tylma – Chambermaid at the King's Fortress in Eregon
- Umdai – Fourteen-year-old daughter of Kellin who befriends Wilby
- Wilby – Fourteen-year-old girl from Eregon, with the mission to restore the Rainbow's End
- Wozner – Son of the Grand Viceroy Trentham and best friend of Jahaamaa

We're forever a family, we're born of God's grace.
We join hands as children from each land and race,
We believe in God's promise that all will be one.
We're a family together, united by love.

We sit at one table, we eat of one bread.
Our hope is in Jesus, by Him we are fed.
We'll dine at one banquet when day's end has come,
Knead your family together, unite us in love.

We're adopted and grafted into Jesus the vine,
As branches that bear fruit, we become God's wine
That flows in abundance from a blessing cup,
Drink as family together united by love.

We pray for the freedom to make all war cease:
A people, a planet where all live for peace.
A springtime of newness with a rainbow above
Like a meadow of color – Unite us in love.

So let's join together, to give thanks and praise:
The God of all loving through wonderful ways
Has made us a people, where each one belongs,
We're a family together united by love.

(Excerpted from the song, *Forever a Family*, (c) 1998, 2022 Dave Pipitone)

THANKS

I am so grateful to God for the guidance, inspiration, and resources to dream and write this book and to all of those who have touched my life, especially these family members: my wife Cheryl and daughter Emily; my Grandparents Tony and Lenora Pipitone, Frank and Mary Libera, my Pipitone family: Mom and Dad (Joel and Cele), my siblings and their spouses and families: Kathy and John, Jennie, Jason and Justin Martin, Gary, Sue and, Thomas Pipitone, Paul, Mary, and Timmy Pipitone, Mimi and Lyle Rasmussen and their daughters Kelly and Katie, Jeff, Allie, and Tony Pipitone, Jackie and Natalee Parochka, Stephanie and Tim Luker, Joe and Diane, and cousins; my Hetrick family: Bill, Bess, Peter, and Sherry Hetrick; Aggie and Joe Cummins, Don and Virginia Jacobson, Johnny, Brian, Steve and Jody Wenzel, Barb and Sobie Elias; my Libera family: Gigi and Wayne Baker, Helen Libera, Sr. Mary Andrew, Andy, John, Mary, Frank, Alene and Ralph, Matt, Steve, Theresa, Frank, Barb, Larry, Rob, Elizabeth, Johnny, and Andy.

Thanks to those who helped review the final manuscript including Dr. Shannon Karafanda, Peter Pappas, Dawn Mayer (who gave me the first tulip bulb for my personal Hope Patch), Colleen

Boland Sall, Geri Smith, Stephanie Luker, Gary Ten Hoven, Susie Pasche Gjestson, George Manisco, Marian Groff, Sherry Hetrick, Sharon Gordon, Jerry Barrio, and Victoria Hargis.

To my friends and colleagues: Tom and Pat Bouton and family; Tim and Charlene Kryszak family; Nancy and Chuck Jaris and family, my Our Lady of the Assumption and Beloit Catholic High School classmates and teachers, Don and Cathy Gabig, Sr. Marianne Supan, Fr. George Kane, Fr. Pat Brennan, Fr. Terry Keehan, Fr. JohnPaul Cafiero, Fr. Denis Caneiro, Fr. Joe Kruszynski and so many other priests; Sr. Mary Southard CSJ, Sr. Irene McCarthy OP, Bill, Ray, Kathy, Denise and Gary, Michaela, Mariah; Joe, Keith, Frank and Charlie; Elizabeth, Allen, Ruth, Carole, Sr. Joanne Marie, Michele, Lisa, Michelle, Marge, Cindy and Ron, Stacey, Michael; Barbara, Don, Gerry, Geri, Skip and Margie, Daryl and Marian, Mike and Nata, Pauline, Ray, Veronica, Kevin, Tom, the three Freds, Joe and Myra, Lynn, Jill, Jason, Tammy, Greg, Julie, Ed, Ruth, Carrie, Brad, Cynthia, Ashiq, Sharon, Patty, Laura, Cheryl, Ronnett, William, Hope, Roger, Jim, Diane, Roger and Kristin, Rick, Monica, Xavier and Cecilia, George and Nancy M., Sr. Mary, Teri, Irene, Skip, Jack, John, Tom, Lori, Bill and Judy K. and their grandchildren Joe and Sam, Brian and Natalie Page, my Knights of Columbus brothers, Dean-o, Bob, the two Toms, Jim, John, and to the litany of thousands of people who live in love and truth.

About the Author

Dave Pipitone is an author, husband, father, and retired market researcher. He wrote the original version of *The Rainbow Chronicles* in the early 2000s and published the first edition in 2004.

Dave has written a series of books about treasuring God and others in different life circumstances which can be found on Amazon.com and at his website, www.transforminglifepress.com

Dave would appreciate your stories, feedback, and suggestions about this book and how it was a benefit to you. If you found a bug (typo, mistake, etc.), we apologize in advance. Please let us know about that, too, so we can fix it. You can contact Dave by email at dave@transforminglifepress.com.

Made in the USA
Columbia, SC
20 April 2022